Hell Ship

Benedict J. Jones

SINISTER
HORROR
COMPANY

PRESENTS

BENEDICT J. JONES

HELL SHIP

Edited by Daniel Marc Chant & J. R. Park
Interior design by Daniel Marc Chant & J. R. Park
Cover design by Vincent Hunt

Published by The Sinister Horror Company

HELL SHIP -- 1st ed.
ISBN 978-1-912578-06-1

ACKNOWLEDGEMENTS

Huge thanks must go to Anthony Watson for all his help in getting Hell Ship afloat, as with most of my books his help behind the scenes is hugely appreciated; thanks mate!

Big love to Justin and Dan at the Sinister Horror Company for believing in the book and making Hell Ship a reality.

Thank you to Lisa; my partner, lover and best friend, for keeping me sane in this crazy world, for making me believe, and for completing me.

As ever thank you to the readers, this was always for you.

For Geraldine, my sister. Gone too soon. I wish you could've read this one.

PROLOGUE

The Malacca Straights February 1944

They were down in the belly of the beast. Down where the heat was a tangible being, a physical entity that weighed on the men and crushed the life from out of them. The only sounds were the murmurs of hopelessness and the clunk-clunk of the engines punctuated by the occasional wail of the lost. Of smells, there were many; sweat, diesel, corruption, rot, and the meaty scent of death.

Whatever cargo the ship had once carried, its load was now one of human misery. Where once perhaps sacks of grain or crates of fruit had lain men were now packed in tighter than cattle on their way to market. Men lay atop other men, limbs twisted and combined forming one, great, panting, mass of sweating flesh. Wide, frightened eyes, stared out. They were filthy, rail thin, and they stank. They had stank for so long now that none of them seemed to notice. They had bigger worries weighing upon their shoulders than the mere fact that they stank.

'Peter is dead.'

Captain Bill Nunhead looked over at his friend Lawrence Cort-Smith, likewise a Captain. Peter Herring had been with them since Singapore when they had been captured in the relentless advance of the Imperial Japanese forces. Since then they had seen prison cells, work camps, and death. Despite it all Nunhead had been convinced that their trio, the three musketeers as they had dubbed themselves, would see the end of the war. That they would see it together and that they would survive. If he could have cried, he would have but having lost so much moisture through sweating and dehydration Nunhead simply did not have the ability to cry. Cort-Smith grasped Nunhead's shoulder, so bony now, and forced a smile.

'He's better off out of it. Have you worked out where the bastards are taking us?'

Nunhead shook his head.

'Another work camp most likely, but where? I don't know and I'm not sure it matters anymore – does it? It'll just be another place where they try to work us to death.'

'Then we try to make a break for it. I'd rather die a free man in the bush than live another moment under their yoke.'

Nunhead smiled despite himself. He looked at Cort-Smith and tried to picture him as he was before – the darling of the officer's mess and always caught up in the social whirl of colonial life. Truth be told they had not been friends until after their capture. Nunhead had never liked the handsome young officer; a charming blonde demon at the pony club and with the young ladies when he wasn't riding. But now, now Nunhead would have given his right arm to make sure that Cort-Smith saw the end of this terrible world that they had found themselves caught up in.

Suddenly there was light in the darkness. A hatch had been thrown open. Men recoiled from the daylight like ghouls in a crypt exposed to the rays of the sun. Nunhead squinted at the light and saw four silhouettes moving down the stairs.

'What do these Johnnies want?'

Once the guards had stepped down into the murk they were easy to see; khaki jackets, shorts, and caps, rifles, with long bayonets attached, in their hands. Men lying near the stairs reached out to them.

'Water…'

'Mercy…'

Rifle butts lashed out, fingers and arms were broken and smashed. One of the guards jabbed out with his bayonet and the men huddled in together even closer than they were before. They had learned to fear the casual cruelness of their captors. The guards looked around at the men, they looked back over their shoulders and Nunhead watched as another man descended into the hold; olive green jacket with a crisp white shirt beneath, white pith helmet, khaki jodhpurs, polished oxblood cavalry boots, and a riding crop tucked under his arm. Like the guards he looked over the prisoners, and then nodded. The guards were spurred to action and used their bayonets to divide ten men out from the crowd and herd them up the stairs. The officer turned to follow.

3

'*Yoroshiku onegai shimasu*,' an English officer, Nunhead recognised him as Major Haddenfield, had spoken in rushed Japanese and stepped from out of the huddle. He was tall, and as thin as the rest, clad in a filthy loincloth and the remnants of a battledress jacket, 'Please, where are you taking these men?'

The Japanese officer considered the Englishman for a moment. When he replied, it was in halting English.

'Where they go is not your concern. You will soon see.'

'*Arigato*,' replied Haddenfield, 'we need water, please.'

'*Arigato*...' the Japanese rolled the word around in his mouth and then smiled at the Major. His riding crop lashed out splitting the skin of Haddenfield's cheek. '*Arigato, arigato*,' he laughed and raised the riding crop again. Haddenfield cowered like a whipped dog. The Japanese Officer laughed again and then followed his men up the stairs.

With a metallic clank the hatch was shut and once again they were in darkness with only the moaning of the dying and the clunk-clunk of the engine.

* * *

The guards came again four more times in the next ninety minutes. The men below decks could hear nothing of what occurred above – just the clunk-clunk of the engine drowning out almost everything else. When they came down the fifth time there were perhaps a third of the men left. Nunhead and Cort-Smith were caught up in the herding and driven towards the stairs.

'Stay close to me, Bill,' whispered Cort-Smith.

They knew enough to let themselves be driven by the guards, any attempt at disobedience or dragging of your feet would earn you a smash from the rifle butts – or worse, and both men knew how long it took them to heal now, they had seen men wither and die from the injuries inflicted off-hand by the guards; broken bones leading to sepsis and shallow bayonet cuts becoming infected and maggot ridden.

The daylight forced them to keep their heads down and eyes away from the glare of the sky. But the air, the air was glorious out of the cargo hold. Both men sucked in great lungfuls of the ocean air. The group of ten were shoved out further on to the deck. Nunhead risked a look up and saw that part of the rail had been removed at the side of the ship, the deck around it was slick with crimson.

'My God…'

Two burly bare-chested Japanese stood waiting, swords in one hand and blood stained rags in the other. There was a shrill cry from behind them and a young Canadian soldier broke clear of the ring of guards and made a break for the rail on the opposite side.

There was the bark of an order and two shots rang out. They watched the Canadian skid and fall, shot through both legs. The Japanese officer pointed his riding crop at the fallen man and shouted. Two soldiers ran forward with thin rope, not much thicker than cord, in their hands. The other nine men watched as the soldiers tied the Canadian's arms together and to his body in a series of ever more complex knots. Once they were done they dragged him over through the gore to the open rails. He was punched until he knelt, forehead touching the deck. One of the burly executioners stepped forward and planted his feet. The katana was brought up and the other soldiers watching took in a breath as one. The blade dropped and the Canadian's head rolled away like a melon falling from a fruit stall. The second swordsman picked up the head and dropped it in a basket while the first used his foot to roll the decapitated soldier to the side. Another kick and he went over, disappearing from view with a splash into the sea. The man who had kicked him over turned and smiled at those who remained as he used the rag to wipe clean the blade of his sword.

'This is murder, murder plain and simple,' muttered Nunhead.

'And what they've been doing to us these last two years wasn't?'

Nunhead had to concede Cort-Smith's point, but this was different. Another man was pulled from the group and the process was repeated. The complex knots, the dragging through the spilt blood and then the beheading.

'Looks like this is it, old man.'

'How can you be so bloody blasé about this?'

'Oh, I'm not, Bill. But I am resigned to it – and at least it's clean. I'd much rather die clean, I decided on that a long time ago but I've never been brave enough to see it through.'

Nunhead looked around; he could see the officers of the ship watching through the windows of the bridge, up to the higher deck where the officer in the pith helmet stood watching and it was then that he saw the figure who stood next to the officer. He was shorter than the officer and slightly bent, as though he had a partial hunch, his face was hidden in the shadows cast from his conical hat. He was clad in robes of so dark a blue that they were almost black, a string of prayer beads as large as golf balls was hanging down from his neck, and he leant on a long thin staff. In this world of machines, guns, soldiers, and uniforms the man stood out as an anachronism who looked like he belonged in some earlier century, whispering advice in the ear of a Shogun or Daimyo, a Samurai lord's religious advisor.

The guards grabbed at Cort-Smith and the blonde officer seemed intent to go quietly but Nunhead could not accept his friend's acquiescence. He stepped forward from the side and drove his head into the guard's face. Nunhead grunted in grim satisfaction as he felt the man's nose break and he grabbed for the rifle. There was shouting one of the other guards stabbed out with his bayonet which bit into Nunhead's side. The scream of his friend drove Cort-Smith to action. He brought his knee up hard into the guard's groin and then punched him in the throat. Weak as it was the blow choked away the guard's breath and the Japanese soldier threw his hands up to his throat letting go of his rifle.

Nunhead struggled for the rifle of his guard and Cort-Smith scooped the fallen weapon up from the deck, working the bolt as he did so. He turned and shot the guard that Nunhead was struggling with through the head. Nunhead's heart rose. They had a chance, slim as it was. Bang-bang-bang; three shots in swift succession. Cort-Smith coughed and stumbled forward. The officer with the riding crop stood above them with his Nimbu pistol in his hand, smoke rising from the barrel. Nunhead swung the rifle determined to avenge his fallen friend. Something hard smashed into his temple and the world span. His legs went from under him and Nunhead hit the deck. He looked across at Cort-Smith and watched the light go out of his eyes. Nunhead sobbed and when he was picked up he did not struggle.

When they tied the knots around his wrists and body the ropes cut into him and burned his flesh. Then he was up and being dragged over to the side. Cort-Smith had said at least it was clean this way and Nunhead found himself agreeing with his friend as he was pinned to the deck. The katana went up and then came down. Another head in a basket, another body as shark bait, the circle continues.

The officer and the priest watched the sky; shapes swirled behind the blue and the sky began to change and twist as though other skies were pressing at it from behind. The blue seemed to bulge, darker colours trying to show through. The priest turned to look at the soldier.

'Yori oku no dansei.' *More men.*

The officer nodded and thunder broke somewhere in the distance.

CHAPTER ONE

Dark. Wet. Cold. Cold enough to steal the breath from your lungs – and it does. You go under and taste salt. Fight your way back to the surface and blink the seawater from your eyes. The sky above you is as dark as the water beneath. You wonder if the tattoos on your feet will do their jobs; a pig on the top of your right foot and a chicken atop the left. Everyone knows that pigs and chickens can't swim, even God, and if he were to look down and see those ink animals on your feet you hope he would take mercy and put you down on land.

The sky above you is lit suddenly, a flare from your ruined ship that lies behind you. How long till it goes down? Machine parts in the hold so it could be mere minutes. You push away trying to put some distance between yourself and the broken ship that you called home. The waves are choppy and high. One raises above you and then crashes down like a cleaver onto a butcher's block pushing you towards the deep.

Break free of the icy fingers clutching at your limbs and drag a breath into your lungs. That's two. You go under the third time and you don't come back up. Everyone knows that. What was it that got you; submarine, mine, raider, some terrible mechanical fault with the engines? Does it matter? You are in the water now, the dark water, and alone on the grace of God.

The moonlight plays across something and you strain your neck like the turtles you saw in the Seychelles, desperate to see, to believe. Yes, yes, it is. A boat. Some bastard, some glorious bastard must have managed to launch a boat before the ship tilted. You've been in the water before. Made it to a boat then and you can make it to the boat again.

Arms like lead now but you swing them, no pretence at technique, and try to crawl through the blackness towards the boat. You kick your legs desperate to stay on the surface, fearing what may lie below (crucifixes inked on the soles of your feet to ward them off).

The sea is your enemy tonight; for every stroke of your arms the water pushes you back three. You kick and fight, claw at the ocean and try to drag yourself through it. Risk a look for the boat and see that it is further away than when you started. Whisper a prayer to God and another to Neptune – it always pays to hedge your bets.

The boat drops away over a wave and you see the wall of blackness coming for you. As it rises above you the fight goes out of your limbs, easier to rest now and let this take its course. You wish you had never made it off the ship, wish you didn't know how to swim, wish that you hadn't even tried.

* * *

Five souls sat in the jolly boat and watched the Empire Carew burn. Occasionally the fires would flare and light up the sky above them. The jolly boat was a decent enough size, space for around thirty people at a push. A young man in a white double-breasted officer's jacket and white cap looked around him at those in the boat with him; a deckhand he vaguely recognised, Putner from the radio room, one of the black lads from the kitchens, and a young woman he guessed was one of the small contingent of Australian nurses which they had been carrying as well as the cargo of machine parts.

While most of them watched the Empire Carew list and burn, Dan Connelly watched the sea. He watched the black mirror like surface for signs of life. It didn't take him long to find some. Far out he could see a man swimming and pulling something with him. It took a moment to realise that the shape he was dragging through the water was another man.

'There! Pass me a hook.'

The young man dressed in white stayed still and looked around as though confused by what a hook was. The black man who Connelly knew as Earl Hamilton picked up one of the long boathooks and passed it over to him.

'We ain't got no light to put on him.'

'Don't want one if that sub is still about,' replied Connelly.

'A sub? Is that what it was?' asked the young officer, Dennis Snell.

The swimmer had closed the distance to the boat. In the dark it was hard to make out who he was. Connelly leaned over the side and Hamilton grabbed his belt so that he wouldn't slip into the ocean beyond.

'Grab the hook.'

The swimmer looked up as though surprised to find other people out here in the dark on the sea. But the man said not a word and just reached up and caught the haft of the boat hook in a solid grip to pull himself, and the man he was pulling, closer to the boat.

'Get him out first,' said the newcomer, voice as rough as old wooden decks. 'Careful with him, the fire caught him.'

Putner, the radio operator, and the young nurse helped to pull the injured party into the boat. Connelly looked at him as he passed; dark hair frazzled down against his skull, the flesh of his ears twisted and malformed like the wax of a well-used candle, the shoulders and back of his shirt blackened and melted into his skin, the man's eyes flickered but he seemed to be in another place.

Once the wounded man was aboard, Connelly reached down and dragged the swimmer over the side. The man pushed himself up from the floor and sat himself down. They could all see that he was spent.

He wore only trousers, his chest a mass of tattoos; compasses, anchors, swallows, golden dragons, and a fully masted ship.

His shoulders and forearms were likewise marked; jaguar on his left forearm and a naked woman on the right, HOLD across the knuckles of his right hand and FAST across the left.

He caught his breath and looked up at Connelly.

'Thanks for the help, Professor.'

Connelly smiled, recognising Royston Busby, the strong arm Donkeyman who kept the Somali Arabs on the black gang down in the Engine Room in line.

'No problem, Busby. That Collins you dragged in with you?'

Busby shrugged his substantial shoulders.

'Man owes me money, couldn't leave him to burn.'

Connelly clapped a hand on Busby's shoulder and turned to look at Collins who had been laid down. The young nurse was crouched over him.

'Miss...sorry I didn't catch your name in all the commotion.'

The dark-haired nurse looked up at Connelly and forced a smile.

'Starling, Amelia Starling.' She held out her hand and Connelly shook it gladly.

'What are his chances?'

'If he's still with us come dawn then he has a chance. Depends if we've got any medical supplies.'

Connelly looked around.

'Reckon you can check on that, Hamilton?'

The man nodded in response.

'Sure, I make an inventory of what we got – and what we lacking.'

'Lacking a bloody smoke right now,' threw in Busby.

'You can smoke when the sun comes up and when we know that we're clear of any Jap subs that are lurking about.'

Busby turned to Snell and saluted.

'Aye-aye, sir.'

'Some more, that is, I can see some more people.'

They all turned to where Putner pointed and saw that the young radio operator was right. Two more swimmers were making for the boat. Hamilton hefted the boat hook and prepared to help bring them in. Connelly returned the favour and took a hold on the waistband of his trousers to stop him pitching forward. The boat was rocked by a swell and Hamilton almost went face first into the water. Connelly grunted and pulled him back.

Once the two people had been pulled up into the boat Connelly looked them over. A man and a woman. The man; balding, somewhere in his late thirties, wearing beige suit trousers and a white shirt, smile on his face once he hit the deck. The woman was blonde, pretty, her patterned dress torn. Connelly recognised them as part of the contingent of passengers they had been shipping along with the nurses and cargo.

'So here we are,' said the man with a smile. 'I'm Conrad Warner and this is the one and only Lily Cecil – songbird of the forces.'

'Stick a sock in it, Conrad,' replied the woman from the deck as she lay back on her elbows like some reclining mermaid, albeit one with a strong cockney accent.

Connelly looked over the people in the jolly boat and then away to where the Empire Carew had been a few moments earlier. The ship was gone and they were alone on the dark water.

CHAPTER TWO

Dawn coloured the sky early in the Indian Ocean. No one in the boat had slept except for Collins, but his fevered dreams could hardly be termed sleep. Connelly scanned the empty horizon.

'If there's no sign of that Nip sub then I'll take that smoke now.'

Connelly turned to look at Busby and then smiled. He reached into his pocket and took out a sealskin tobacco pouch. He passed it over to Busby.

'Roll me one while you're at it, would you?'

'You can roll your bloody own, Professor – what am I your flunky wallah?'

Busby rolled himself a cigarette and then passed the pouch back to let Connelly roll his own.

'Got a match?'

Connelly looked at him in disbelief but then handed over his box of Swan Vestas. Busby lit his own smoke and then stood to light Connelly's from the same match.

'What's the course then?'

'I think I'll be the judge of that.'

Busby looked over at Snell who sat watching him, double-breasted jacket hanging open now, white shirt and black tie beneath.

'That right, *sir*?'

'I don't like your tone, Busby.'

Busby smirked.

'Funny that, seeing as I don't like getting told what to do by a jumped-up little cabin boy.'

'Busby…'

'Stay out of this, Professor, let the boy answer for himself.'

Snell coloured, red rising to his cheeks in stark contrast to the grubby white of his uniform.

'I am the ranking officer on this boat.'

'Wouldn't be an officer at all if it weren't for your daddy is what I heard. Wouldn't have even got a berth on the Carew if Captain Wingrove hadn't been your bloody uncle or whatever.'

'The Captain was my godfather,' whispered Snell, 'and he's dead. You will obey my orders or there will be a reckoning.'

'A reckoning?' Busby puffed away on his cigarette and snorted, enjoying himself.

The rest of the boat's party looked on.

'You reckon you can navigate us out of here, eh? Which way is it to Ceylon then?'

Snell looked confused. He looked around. Up at the sky, the horizon, the sun.

'I…that is, I think…'

'You think? It's that way, that's the way to Colombo,' said Busby pointing away to starboard. 'Way I see it is this; you sit down over there and let those that know run this boat the way it needs to be run, there's a good little *gentleman*.'

Busby was swaggering now seeing that the fight and argument seemed to have fallen away from the younger man. Busby had never liked officers and this was his chance to really stick it to one. Connelly threw a look over at the boathook. He looked up and saw Hamilton staring back at him. The black man considered him for a moment and then nodded. Connelly was just about to reach for the hook when Snell spoke again.

'There is one thing, Busby. One thing that might persuade you of my authority.'

'And what's that?' replied Busby jutting his chin out, cock of the walk now.

The young cadet officer reached into the pocket of his jacket. When his hand re-emerged it held a short barrelled Webley Mark V .455 revolver, nickel plated. He held it loosely but the business end was pointed straight at Busby's gut and the threat was clear.

'Well, there is this… my godfather made sure I took it when he told us to take the boat and my *daddy* made sure I knew how to use one before I left England so you will obey me, Mr Busby, or I will have you hog tied until we make landfall – do I make myself clear?'

Connelly saw Busby's right hand slipping around behind his back. He had seen the move before in bars from New Orleans to Manilla. Busby smiled and nodded all the while he was reaching for the seven-inch switchblade he kept cached at his back. Connelly stepped forward and caught Busby's wrist. He turned it on its self and kept the pressure up as he spoke.

'I think Royston was just a little worse for wear, Mr Snell. He's just concerned we all get home safe. I'm sure he didn't mean anything by it.'

Snell watched Connelly for a moment, searching his eyes for some kind of connection, and then nodded.

'Of course – say no more about it, shall we? Mr Busby, thank you for pointing out the right direction to me, I bow to your superior knowledge. Would you be so good as to run up the sail and take first watch pointing us correctly?'

Connelly released Busby's wrist. The bigger man turned to look at him. They stared dead into each other's eyes and then Busby smiled. It was not a smile that Connelly enjoyed seeing.

'My pleasure, sir.'

Busby set to work running up the small sail and Connelly breathed a sigh of relief. He looked over to Hamilton and nodded but knew that Busby would want to *discuss* the issue with him at some point.

'Did you manage to make that inventory?'

'Sure did.'

'Then I'm sure Mr Snell would appreciate it if you could advise him on it.'

'Sir,' said Hamilton to Snell and the young officer nodded in return, 'we got the canvas sail that's getting run up now, six pairs of oars, a compass, sea anchor, boat cover, an axe, some flares along with some matches, a medical kit I gave to Miss Starling, and the two boat hooks.'

'Food and water?' asked Snell.

'Got us a four-gallon pot of water, eleven tins of condensed milk, one twenty-pound tin of ships biscuits and about sixteen pounds of tinned mutton – I think that even I will struggle to turn that into anything palatable.'

Snell looked around the boat and the passengers and crew looked back at him. Connelly could see the calculations working in the officer's brain; nine people in the boat came out at about two pounds of biscuits and nearly the same of mutton each, less than half a gallon of water each.

'Half a cup of water all round, sir?' asked Connelly.

'What? Why, yes, yes of course. Half-a-cup each and a biscuit each to serve as breakfast.'

'Best we rig up the boat cover to try and catch any rain if it does come – and set it at night to catch the dew. Might be we'll be glad of it.'

Snell swallowed. Hard. Not wanting to think beyond their meagre supplies, hoping they would be picked up before it came to that.

'Thank you, Mr, err, Connelly?'

'Yes, sir. Connelly.'

'Why does Busby call you Professor?'

'Because he saw me read a book once.'

Busby laughed from the back of the boat where he sat at the rudder.

'That ain't the half of it.'

* * *

Earl Hamilton leaned back against the slats that formed the side of the boat and tried to chew a little life into the hard ship's biscuit. He sighed and thought of home – grilled red snapper and buttered cassava. Looked up at the bright blue sky and could almost believe he was back in Barbados rather than bobbing around the Indian

Ocean in this toy tub. Get to see his wife and boy again, it had been too long. He took a mouthful from his half cup of water, wished for a cold beer, and then broke off another piece of biscuit which he put into his mouth along with the water to try and soften it up some.

'Do you think we will get picked up?'

'Huh?'

Hamilton looked around and found Putner, the radio operator, sitting next to him.

'I said do you reckon that we'll get picked up?'

'I don't know. Who can tell? Ask those guys they look like they've been adrift before?'

Putner looked over at Busby and then to Connelly. To him they looked like proper sailors; not afraid of anything; hard living, hardworking, and as tough as the ships they served on. Putner had never felt tough, more comfortable with his radios, codes, and electrics than with people.

'I hope we do.'

He looked over at Hamilton and the other man nodded before chewing on his still hard biscuit with a sigh.

Across the boat from Hamilton and Putner sat Conrad Warner and Lily. Warner reached into his back pocket and extracted a gold cigarette case.

'You reckon they're still dry?'

'Man who sold it to me promised it was waterproof. Course it could be he was a liar and a flim-flam salesman but there's only one way to find out…'

'Suck it and see?' replied Lily.

Warner looked at her and smiled.

'Wish you would.'

'Oi,' she dug her elbow into Warner's ribs but there was no real violence in it.

Warner opened the cigarette case and smiled. Its precious cargo was safe and dry. He took out his lighter and tried to spark it. It wouldn't and he sighed.

'Anyone spare a chap a match?'

'Trade you a couple for one of those tailor mades,' replied Connelly and Warner held up the case.

Lily and Conrad lit their smokes from the same match but Connelly extinguished it and used another to light his own.

'Sorry, sailor's superstitions.'

Then Connelly passed another three matches to Warner which he tucked into his pocket.

'Thanks,' said Lily and Connelly gave her a nod. 'This happened to you before?'

'Twice. Hit one of our own mines running a cargo of rubber out from Rangoon but we got in the boats in plenty of time, picked up two days later. The other time was near Madagascar, U-Boat caught us without a destroyer in sight. We were in the water for twelve hours before a ship got to us. Saw some good men pulled under.'

'Jesus,' muttered Lily.

'Sharks?' asked Warner and Connelly simply nodded, his mind back treading water and waiting to die in the clear African sea.

* * *

'Margie, that you Margie?'

Amelia Starling dipped the rag over the side into the sea water and used it to wet Collin's brow. He moaned as the wet cloth touched his forehead. Amelia sniffed hard. There was little she could do for the man with what was in the small medical kit that had been stowed in the boat. There was no morphine and that, she knew, was what the man needed. Instead all she could do was sit with him and wait for the burns to do their worst.

'Penny for 'em?'

Amelia looked around at the blonde woman who had come and sat beside her. The woman took the cigarette out from between her lips and passed it to Amelia.

'Sorry, I don't really smoke.'

'It ain't for you, love – it's for him.'

The nurse tucked the cigarette between Collins' lips and the man took a deep, automatic, drag. He held it for a moment and then released the smoke in a long stream with an audible sigh of pleasure. Amelia passed the cigarette back and Lily took a final pull on it before casting it away into the sea.

'I'm Lily. Reckon us girls need to stick together on this little jaunt. Where you from?'

'Little town called Nelson, about fifty miles from Darwin. You?'

'Stepney, love. East End of London. How comes you ended up in all this?'

'I've got a brother in the army. It didn't seem right that I just sat back on the farm and did nothing while all those lads were doing their best to stop the Germans and the Japanese.'

Lily nodded.

'I had a brother. Killed in the desert. This fucking war…'

Amelia blanched at the language and Lily laughed.

'Sorry, love. Too much time around soldiers and sailors – and before that I helped my old dad in his pub. Maybe one day I'll sing for some of the RAF boys and then I'll have to mind my Ps and Qs,' she winked at Amelia and the nurse couldn't help but laugh.

'What is it you do?'

'Oh, I sing; radio, concerts, wherever I get sent, try to keep the boys spirits up,' she turned her head and gestured at Conrad Warner. 'We passed through South Africa and then did a couple of dates in your neck of the woods. We were meant to be on our way to Ceylon and then on to India. Connie's my agent, my manager, all of that. He says after the war is done he'll be able to get me some proper gigs and make sure we can see some money.'

'It sounds nice.'

Lily shrugged.

'It is what it is I suppose. It beats living off ration books and black market meat back in Stepney.'

'Gis a song,' shouted Busby from his place back at the rudder.

Lily smiled.

'My audience awaits, help me out if you can.'

And then she began to sing.

'When they begin the beguine,

It brings back the sound of music so tender,

It brings back a night of tropical splendour,

It brings back a memory ever green.'

Faltering at first Amelia added her voice to Lily's and Busby gave a clap of delight.

'I'm with you once more under the stars,

And down by the shore an orchestra's playing,

And even the palms seem to be swaying,

When they begin the beguine.
To live it again is past all endeavour,
Except when that tune clutches my heart,
And there we are, swearing to love forever,
And promising never, never to part.

What moments divine, what rapture serene,
Till clouds came along to disperse the joys we had tasted,
And now when I hear people curse the chance that was wasted,
I know but too well what they mean;
So don't let them begin the beguine,
Let the love that was once a fire remain an ember;
Let it sleep like the dead desire I only remember,
When they begin the beguine.
Oh yes, let them begin the beguine, make them play,
Till the stars that were there before return above you,
Till you whisper to me once more,
'Darling, I love you!'
And we suddenly know, what heaven we're in,
When they begin the beguine…'

Amelia's cheeks glowed red as the rest of the boat clapped. Lily gave a little bow of her head before speaking.

'Course, when Cole Porter wrote that I think 'e was on something of a different sort of cruise to the one we've ended up on…'

CHAPTER THREE

The water lasted three days. The cigarettes and tobacco ran out on the same day as the water. The mutton lasted them four and the biscuits five days. The condensed milk kept them alive while they waited for the rain.

The clouds grew thick and heavy above them and they waited. And waited. Lips chapped and split, skin becoming hot and dry to the touch like ancient papyrus left out in the desert. They prayed and they cursed but the sky just would not break no matter how much it threatened. Until then all they had was the dew that they collected each morning from the boat cover.

'Almost like we got a Jonah on this boat...' said Busby throwing a look at Snell but there was no real malice in his words, he just wanted someone to bite and give him an argument to break the monotony.

No one took him up on his offer.

Hamilton and Warner talked about music, jazz mostly. Lilly and Amelia kept close company. Busby watched Snell and Snell watched Busby. Collins moaned and begged to die. Putner kept to himself and Connelly wished that he had something, anything, to read.

'What I wouldn't give for a gin,' said Lily.

Warner smiled.

'At the Café Du Paris.'

'Oh, naturally,' replied Lily.

'Cold beer for me,' threw in Connelly, 'so cold it makes the glass of the bottle sweat.'

'Bottle of Cutty Sark,' Busby.

'Rum,' Hamilton.

'Beer for me too,' Putner.

'You don't like beer. Have a lemonade,' Busby again.

'I do to, I like a beer.'

'Let him have a beer if he wants beer,' said Connelly, 'and I'll have another.'

'Champagne all round.'

Lily looked at Warner.

'You finally standing a round then, Connie?'

Warner gave her a wink.

'We get out of here, kid and I promise the drinks are on me.'

'Best make that two bottles of Cutty Sark then.'

'For you Busby – of course! Maybe a woman as well?'

Busby closed his eyes and groaned.

'Don't get me started on women. There's some little chippies in Colombo that'll make your toes curl back up on themselves with what they can do with their mouths…'

'Busby…' threw in Snell but it was a half-hearted reprimand. 'For me it'd have to be a sandwich.'

The others all looked at him, rapt.

'What kind?' asked Warner, sitting up.

'Ham, sliced off a big hunk that's been roasted with honey and cloves – the way my mother used to do it. Cheese, Cheddar, big slices of the stuff. Lashings of mustard and lots of butter. White, door step bread – rations be damned!'

Busby laughed.

'Pickled onions on the side?'

'Hardly a ham sandwich without,' replied Snell, a smile on his lips.

'Oysters,' threw in Warner.

'Oh no,' replied Amelia, 'nothing from out of the sea – a big fat steak, rare as you like and dripping with essence so you need a piece of bread just to mop up the plate after.'

Connelly's mouth watered at the thought.

'And all on Conrad!'

'Drinks, I said drinks – you can all buy your own food.'

'Cheapskate.'

'Well, I ain't Rockefeller.'

The talk stopped and they were all left with their thoughts. And then a drop of rain fell, then another.

'Get the water pot!'

'Make sure the cover is up.'

'Get your cups out.'

'Open your mouths and turn 'em skyward!'

The rain fell hard and heavy. While the others filled their cups as best they could, Busby leant over the side and slipped his hands into the water. A moment later he flipped a large fish into the boat.

'Finish that off for me,' Busby said to Putner.

The young radio operator looked at a loss and then Hamilton slammed the butt end of one of the hooks down onto the fish's head. Busby tossed another into the boat. Everyone waited with baited breath as he repeated the feat for a third time like a magician producing rabbit after rabbit from out of a top hat. Everyone stared at Busby in amazement.

'They like the rain, makes 'em come up,' Busby said with shrug and then took out his knife, popped the blade, and began to gut and clean the fish.

They cooked the fish in the cans left over from the biscuits and mutton. They ate well and washed down with a quarter-cup of water each. The water pot was half-full again and the crew of the jolly boat was sated. For the moment, at least.

CHAPTER FOUR

Day nineteen. No water for three days, no food for four.

The seagull sat on the end of the boat. It looked around and then let out a loud squawk. Connelly crept forward another inch, in his hands a rough lasso spliced together from the boat's line. He took a breath and knew that the others watching him had taken the same breath and held it tight in their lungs just as he did. He tossed the rope noose for the bird's neck and missed. He watched as the gull hopped a few inches further along the edge of the boat. The bird turned and regarded him with a cold glance, its wings twitched as though it were about to take flight.

The gunshot shattered the silence and took off the gull's head. The body continued to walk for a moment and then keeled over into the boat.

Connelly threw a look back to see Snell aiming his Webley along the boat.

'We couldn't lose another one. We just couldn't.'

Busby dragged himself up and retrieved the bird. He lifted it high and let the blood from its ruined neck drip onto his tongue. He passed the carcass across to Snell.

'I'm not going drink that thing's blood.'

'Yes, you are, *sir*. Because if you don't you will die. Get a few drops down your neck and then let the ladies have some. We all drink the blood and then we roast what's left – we have to.'

Snell tucked the pistol back into the pocket of his trousers and took the proffered bird, squeezing its body slightly so that the blood flowed again from the ruined neck and into his mouth. He swallowed it down and then the bird was passed around.

Everyone's faces and exposed flesh had been beaten by the sun, their lips were split and cut, hair as dry as grass in an area of drought. They hadn't seen hide nor hair of boat nor land. It was as though the great expanse of ocean around them was their entire galaxy and the jolly boat their Earth, their *terra firma*, within it.

* * *

Collins had stopped moaning. He lay and shivered on the deck. Connelly looked him over and then took Amelia to one side.

'How is he still alive?'

'He's strong. We've given him water when we have it, tried to make him eat. But, you're right. By everything I know he should have died a week back, I'm not sure what he's holding on for.'

Connelly shrugged.

'What do any of us hold on for?'

'Nothing waiting for you back in port, sailor?'

'My problem is I always want to see the next port.'

'Nowhere to call home?'

'Maybe once but now my home is whatever ship I'm on for however long I'm on it. Doss houses when I don't have a ship.'

'And how long have you lived like that?'

'Ten years now, give or take.'

'I can't imagine living like that.'

'You like your farm?'

Amelia nodded.

'It's a good place.'

'I've seen good places, bad too. Mostly I just like to keep moving.'

'A woman?'

'Don't all good stories start with one?'

'And he doesn't just call you Professor because you read?'

'No. I managed a year of University.'

'What made you leave?'

'A woman, and then just because I didn't want to go back. I like the places I see – good and bad. Maybe one day I'll stop moving but for now…'

'And the woman?'

Connelly gave her a rueful smile.

'Who knows. Married most likely with a score of kids and a little house. It doesn't matter anymore, maybe it never did.'

Amelia smiled and looked away.

'Not something that would interest you then?'

'The house and kids? Perhaps, in a purely academic way of course.'

'Well, of course, Professor.'

'It doesn't sound so bad when you say it.'

'Fog bank rolling in!' shouted Putner breaking into their conversation.

They turned to look and they could see it off across the water; thick, grey, impenetrable. The bank of fog moved closer and then the boat cut into it. Once inside they couldn't see more than half a yard from the boat.

'Keep the hooks ready,' said Connelly, and Hamilton along with Putner grabbed up the boat hooks while Busby kept the tiller pointed dead ahead. Snell moved to the front of the boat and leant forward trying to gain a few extra yards of vision.

Collins' foot suddenly began to trip hammer against the deck. Connelly spun to check the source of the noise and Amelia moved to the side of the burnt mariner. He sat up and his eyes opened, his mouth gasping at the air like a fish out of water.

'Death, we sail with death now. Oh, the blood – blood is the engine, blood is the power, blood is the way!'

'Shut up!' shouted Putner.

'Dead, all dead, we're all dead already. You haven't seen. My God, the things I can see. Better off dead – you're all better off dead!'

Putner turned with the boat hook grasped tightly in his hands.

'Someone shut him up, or I will.'

Connelly grabbed the younger man's shoulder.

'Your job is to keep an eye for anything that might damage the boat. Let Miss Starling deal with Collins. He's just hurting, that's all.'

'There's something out there,' shouted Snell.

Hamilton peered out into the fog where Snell pointed.

'He's right – looks like a ship.'

'Ours?' asked Warner and Lily pushed herself to the front of the boat next to Snell.

'Can't see much of it.'

'Shit, it's better than any more time in this tub,' said Busby. 'Take to the bloody oars and get us closer.'

They broke out the six oars and put them at the ready. Hamilton, Connelly, Putner, and Warner took to the oars while Snell remained aft calling out which way to go. Amelia tried to calm Collins who had laid back down on the decking while Lily stayed at Snell's side.

'Heave to, heave to!' shouted Snell as the brow of the boat almost brushed the side of the ship.

Connelly looked up at the vessel, it looked like an old cargo vessel – a refrigerator ship perhaps or one used for running rubber. It also looked as though the ship had seen better days besmirched as it was by dirt and peeling paint. As the jolly boat slid along the side they could make out the name, obscured as it was by grime and filth, the *Shinjuku Maru*.

'It's a bloody Nip tub!' shouted Busby. 'Snell, you get that bloody pistol out and keep it ready.'

The young officer fumbled the Webley out from his pocket and pointed it up at the ship – the sight of one man with a revolver pointing it at a large ship would have been comical if it were not for the fear on the faces of the rest of the boat's company.

The ship had once been white but now it was stained here and there with rust, apart from that it was filthy as though it had ridden through a dozen storms and had no seamen to give her a good scrub after. Dirt and silt streaked the sides. The decks were quiet and not a soul stirred.

'Do we push off or remain alongside, sir?' asked Hamilton.

Snell looked back at Busby and then swallowed.

'Keep us alongside. We go aboard. If there are Japanese, then we surrender.'

'Not me,' said Busby.

'Nor me,' muttered Connelly. 'And taking the women on board, think about it, sir…'

Snell turned and stared at the men, pistol in his hand pointing at the deck.

'Or what? Take them back out into the ocean and hope we catch another gull? Get us alongside and throw the lines – that's an order.'

The deck above remained quiet.

'Should have seen someone by now.'

Connelly nodded to Hamilton.

'You're right. What do you think Busby?'

'Could be a ghoster. Only one way to know for sure. Toss those lines and get us alongside.'

As he spoke Busby picked up the axe. The lines were thrown and they pulled the jolly boat in tight to the side. Snell moved back down the boat.

'Busby, Connelly, Putner. You three are with me. The rest of you are to remain in the boat. If this goes awry then you cut the lines and push off, try to lose the ship in the fog. Understood?'

Hamilton nodded.

'I hear you, sir.'

With that Snell grasped the ladder and scrambled up it. Busby and his axe followed. Connelly reached into his pocket and withdrew a clasp knife. He extended the four-inch blade and held it between his teeth, pirate-style, as he ascended the ladder. Putner looked at the boat hook for a moment and then left it behind, determining it to be too unwieldy for ascending the ladder, before following.

Benedict J. Jones

CHAPTER FIVE

The deck was as filthy as the exterior of the ship and just as quiet and empty. Nothing stirred. They had climbed aboard at the side of the deck which was covered by another deck overhead, there were doors here and there in the bulkhead of the ship. Busby crept in low against the wall and stared down towards the open foredeck. Connelly likewise kept low and moved up next to him. Putner and Snell ducked down against the railing. Snell waved back to Hamilton.

'What you reckon, Professor – a ghoster?'

'Could be, else they're playing dead on us.'

'Now why would they do that? Tub like this would have a crew of what – thirty, forty? If they were here and they wanted us they could take us.'

'A hundred reasons why. We play it careful and we play it by ear.'

Busby nodded and hefted his axe.

'Fair dos.'

Connelly gestured to Snell and the young officer crabbed across the deck to him.

'Suggestions?'

'We make for the bridge. Take care that there isn't anyone else on board.'

'And if there is?'

'If they're Japs...' began Connelly but Busby interrupted with a gesture – he drew his index finger across his throat and Snell swallowed.

'Keep that pistol ready, but don't you pull that trigger unless you have to. We do this quiet,' Busby paused for a moment, 'sir.'

Snell nodded. Putner moved over to where they were crouched. Busby slipped his hand around his waist and produced his switchblade. He thumbed the catch and the long stiletto blade clicked out and into place.

'Keep that handy, lad. Don't lose it cos I'll be wanting it back.'

Putner looked at the knife in his hand and then back up at Busby.

'If a Jap comes at you then you stick that in his gut and when he grabs the wound you stick it in his neck, savvy?'

Putner gulped and nodded, already praying that the ship was empty.

Connelly took the lead, his knife held low, and Busby followed, then Snell, and finally Putner. The young radio operator sweated as they approached a ladder that led upwards, his hand shook and he looked once more at the lethal blade that Busby had passed to him. He prayed once more that the ship really was a ghoster, like Busby had said, and that no one still lurked in the dark places and hidey-holes on the ship.

The deck they emerged onto was empty. Connelly took a quick look around and then ran to the short ladder that led up to the bridge. Busby followed, staring at the stained deck as he went; at first it looked like rust but on closer consideration the sailor could see that it wasn't rust, something had been spilled across the deck and then washed away by the rain and wind and salt in the sea air. The others followed and they looked up at the heavy door that would lead into the bridge. The door was scarred and buckled, bent as though struck by some huge force.

'Wonder what the hell happened to her?' asked Snell.

'It doesn't matter. Let's get inside and check the bridge – see if we can find the charts, anything.'

'Fuck the charts. It's a drink I'm after – and maybe some vittles.'

Connelly looked at Busby and nodded.

'After you then.'

Busby smiled and cocked the axe back on his shoulder as he moved toward the door. Behind him Snell brought up the Webley and Putner readied his blade, Connelly kept his knife low and prepared himself to leap into the bridge once Busby had breached the door. The big sailor grasped the handle and with a low roar threw it open and leapt inside swinging his axe like some barbarian tribesman leaping amid his enemies. The others followed him in a rush and packed inside the bridge.

There was no one inside. Papers and charts lay here and there, a steel cup sat next to what would have been the captain's chair.

'Found your charts.'

'Have a look around and you might find your drink.'

Putner had sat himself down in a corner, adrenaline fast wearing off and the tiredness of the last few weeks catching up on him in full force. The charts and maps drew Connelly and Snell to them while Busby began to search hoping to find the elusive bottle.

'Will these help?'

Connelly nodded.

'If we can get a more accurate position we might be able to get ourselves in somewhere quicker.'

'Course if the radio was working I could just put out an all-ships distress call.'

They all turned to look at Putner. Busby smiled and nodded at Connelly.

'Surprised you didn't think of that, Professor. Good lad,' he added punching Putner in the shoulder.

'Where are the crew and the captain, do you think?' asked Snell and Busby shrugged.

'Had to abandon the ship for some reason, who knows.'

'Would a captain leave his charts?'

Another shrug from Busby and then the big sailor went back to searching in the drawers. Connelly leaned against the captain's chair and thought on what Snell had said. As he thought he stared out of the window at the fog that shrouded the ship. Above them the fog was darkening, showing a change in the sky that lay beyond it. Lightning flashed somewhere in the distance, lighting up the fog.

'We need to get the boat tied off and everyone on board. If there is a storm coming in, then it is better that we're all on this hulk rather than floating in that little tub.'

'But is it safe?' asked Putner.

'Safe as anywhere else,' muttered Busby.

'No luck finding a dram then?'

'Nah, found you some books though.'

Busby turned and tossed three books at Connelly. He caught them and turned them over in his hands. The first was in Japanese and his heart sank, the second the same. Connelly had enough of the Japanese language to order more beer or ask for a woman but he couldn't read it worth a damn. The third was hand written but was again in Japanese script. Connelly sighed but tucked the leather-bound book into the back of his waistband.

Adjusting the cap on his head Snell looked around and then addressed his men.

'We do as Mr Connelly suggests; secure the boat and get everyone on board. At least it will give us some respite and there may be supplies on board that can sustain us. Are we agreed?'

Busby stood in the doorway and sniffed the air outside.

'Storm coming in all right.'

Putner had got to his feet.

'After, I can see if I can find the radio room – could be one of ours about, or a Yank, or even a neutral ship, something. Anything.'

Snell nodded.

'So we are agreed. Let's get to it.'

* * *

By the time they got back down to where the boat was tied up the rain had started. What they had prayed for in the days previous now became a reality. A reality that blew in hard on a cutting wind and lashed the *Shinjuku*

41

Maru. Not wanting to risk anything from the boat they brought up the oars and other gear that remained for stowing close at hand should they need to return to the jolly boat.

Once the boat was secured with numerous lines, double checked by Busby, the company moved as one and filed inside one of the doors. It led into what looked to have been the main mess for the crew; long tables bolted to the deck, steel cupboards with locks to keep them shut on rough seas, a simple kitchen.

'Give me a hand,' said Hamilton to Warner, 'let's see if there's anything edible in this place.'

Warner nodded and followed the kitchen hand with a smile, happy to be out of the small boat and back on something that resembled safety. Collins was laid down on one of the tables while they tried to decide what to do with him.

'Maybe see if there are some blankets, more medical supplies maybe, something to make him more comfortable – I don't think it will be long now...'

Connelly nodded to Amelia.

'Think we need to send out a scavenging party. Make sure that there isn't anyone else on board as well.'

'Split up?' said Putner and Connelly nodded.

'We need to keep this room secure while we ride the weather out. But in the meantime, you need to get to the radio room, we need to make Collins comfortable, and we need whatever we get from this ship.'

Snell nodded.

'The women, Warner, Hamilton and Collins all stay here. I'll try and find the radio room with Putner, you and Busby go and see what else can be found.'

'Makes sense to me – Busby?'

'Me and you, Professor.'

Snell checked the Webley.

'How many shots you got left?' asked Busby.

'Enough, Mr Busby, enough. Putner, let's try to find this radio room and see if we can get a message out.'

'Just try not to bring any Japs down on us, those little Nip bastards listen in just like everyone else.'

Connelly touched his hand to Busby's elbow.

'Come on, let's see if we can find some morphine for Collins or a bottle of sake for you.'

Busby grinned.

'I haven't had sake since Yokohama,' he looked over at Collins. 'Yeah, we'll get him some blankets and that as well,' he raised his voice, 'you still owe me money Collins, so don't go dying on me!'

Amelia sighed and went back to tending the injured seaman. Hamilton, Warner, and Lily were rifling through the cupboards. Lily stopped and turned.

'Go hunter-gather, we'll try and have something hot waiting for you.'

Busby looked back at her and grinned before Connelly pushed him out of the mess and down a ladder that ran to the lower decks. A moment after, Snell and Putner headed back out onto the rain-lashed deck to hunt out the radio room.

Benedict J. Jones

CHAPTER SIX

The cupboards in the mess gradually gave up their treasure; sacks of rice, jars of pickled vegetables, salt, chillies, two dozen tins of canned fish, another dozen of corned beef, several gallons of water, and two big cans of cooking oil. Hamilton looked over the loot along with the pile of pans and knives they had discovered.

'Looks like pay dirt. We'll eat well once I find out how they work their stove.'

'Not quite champagne and steak but right now I could eat a scabby horse.'

Amelia pulled a face and then laughed.

'No cigarettes though,' said Conrad Warner.

'You need to check the crew's quarters for them,' replied Hamilton.

'Might just have to do that.'

'See if you can find me a comb while you're at it, Connie, I feel like a scarecrow.'

'My pleasure, madam,' said Warner while affecting a bow and kissing Lily's hand.

With that he headed off towards the ladder leading down.

'Hey, man, might be an idea to wait for the others.'

Warner looked back at Hamilton and smiled.

'I'll be fine.'

Hamilton shook his head and then picked up a cleaver from amongst the kitchen knives that they had found. He offered it handle first to Warner.

'Take this with you, just in case.'

Smiling, Warner walked back and took the proffered weapon.

'Really?'

Hamilton dead-eyed him.

'Okay, okay. I'll take it with me, mother hen.'

He laughed and then turned towards the ladder.

'Be careful, Connie.'

'I always am! Back soon.'

* * *

The hallways and passages of the ship were dark. The lights unlit showing that the ship had no power. It rolled in the swell and push of the sea and Snell steadied himself against the wall. He was scared, scared of what they might find in the dark, scared he would let the rest of the company down with a bad decision, and scared that he would not live up to the belief that had been placed in him as an officer.

'This way you think, sir?'

Snell nodded.

'I think so. It has to be this way somewhere if this ship is built like any other that I've been on.'

'Looking forward to getting a look at their radio.'

'Oh?'

'I've been feeling pretty useless, truth be told. Connelly and Busby, they're proper sailors and know what to do. I'm just a radio man – do you know what I mean?'

'Yes, I think I do. How many voyages have you been on?'

'This was my fourth trip.'

In the dark, Snell grimaced, that was three more voyages than he had been on.

'Well, we all have our skills and our berth. Let's find this radio room and then you can show everybody what you can do.'

'Thank you, sir.'

Snell's hand felt sweaty on the hard waffle-pattern of the Webley's grip, He wiped his hand on the cuff of his jacket and then did likewise with the pistol butt. He was glad of the hard, heavy weight in his hand and he thought about what it would be like to fire the bullet into the flesh of another man.

They pushed on along the dark corridor trying to find the right door.

* * *

'First time we been on our own since all this started.'

Connelly looked up at Busby and his hand slipped into his pocket to find the closed clasp knife. He had travelled enough that he was quick with his hands but he had seen Busby brawl and would rather be armed if it came to that; in New Orleans he had seen Busby fight on after a chair had been broken over him and fork stuck into his head. They were in a cabin that looked like it might have belonged to one of the ship's officers. Two bunk beds, metal desk bolted down to the floor and a loose chair – not much to pick up and use if it came to a fracas.

'And you have some things to say do you?'

Busby smiled and then looked down at the deck.

'No – not like that, Professor. I know why you backed Snell up and you were right to do it.'

'Yes?'

Busby nodded.

'Yeah, we make port – and we will, and I've done the officer it'd go badly for me - so thanks. You know me, Professor, they just rile me, officers, especially when they don't know fuck all.'

'Well, that's most of them.'

'Ha! Always liked you, Connelly. Let's get these blankets back to Collins. Keep an eye out for fags or booze though.'

'I always do.'

* * *

Conrad Warner whistled Duke Ellington's *Don't Get Around Much Anymore* as he walked. It was dark below decks, the only light thrown by the occasional porthole. He stopped and looked out of one; rain lashed in off a grey sea, the water looked high and choppy the waves starting to grow higher. Warner reached for his cigarette case and had it half-open before he realised that it was empty.

'Shit,' he swore with a half-smile playing on his lips.

He tried a door and found it locked. The next opened into what looked like the quarters for eight men – four sets of bunkbeds. He looked around and couldn't see much difference between this and the crew quarters he had seen on other ships during his travels. He used the cleaver to smash the locks off of the foot lockers at the ends of the bunkbeds and began to rifle through them; jumpers, spare uniforms, pictures of sweet hearts, and pictures of a more *unclothed* nature from ports around Asia, and cigarettes… Warner smiled. He had hit pay dirt in the first chest – a large carton of Golden Bat cigarettes.

Warner hefted the carton in his hand. He stripped the paper from the top and took a cigarette out. He lit it with the last match in his pocket and enjoyed the taste. Normally he would have tossed a cigarette of this quality but right then it tasted like the best he had ever smoked. It seemed a shame to leave the rest of the foot lockers unsearched and so, with the cigarette stuck to his bottom lip, he went to work. Once Warner had the other lockers open he threw the contents out onto the floor and raked through the contents with the cleaver; more clothes, more cigarettes, two clay bottles that Warner presumed was sake, a bottle of cheap whiskey – Piper's Spirit brand, some chocolate bars, nick-knacks from dozens of ports, letters, and more photographs. He allowed himself a smile at the haul and wrapped it, hobo-like, in a sheet to carry back to the mess room. Lily would be pleased when she saw the cigarettes.

A huge clank made Warner drop his bundle. He turned and held up the cleaver, brandishing it like an irate butcher confronting a meat thief.

'Who's there?'

Warner heard the fear in his own voice. The clank came again, lower this time. Warner stared into the shadows and saw the steam pipes running around the room. He laughed and called himself a fool. The clanking became even lower and more rhythmic. Warner let the cleaver fall to his side and walked over to the pipes. The ship looked like no one had been on it for weeks, months maybe. What the hell was clanking through the pipes; oil, water, filth? Warner stood and stared, not daring to touch any of the valves or handles that were on the pipes.

The clanking came to a stop and Warner took a step closer. Silence. He took another step. There was another sound now. Warner dipped his head trying to make it out more clearly; a hissing, low and almost inaudible. He stared at the valve that seemed to be hissing. The turn ring came loose and shot across the room like a bullet. Warner ducked and when he stood back up, the pipe suddenly sprayed dark ichor into his face. Stumbling back, Warner tried to wipe the liquid from his mouth and nose. He retched against the coppery taste and spat it out onto the deck. Grabbing a sheet he had cast aside from one of the trunks Warner wiped the remainder of the liquid from his face. It was dark and thick like water from the bilges. Warner gave his face another going over with the cloth and then threw it into the corner of the room. He stared at the pipe – silent now – before gathering up his bundle and heading back to the others.

CHAPTER SEVEN

Snell pulled another door open and stepped around it with his arm extended, pistol pointed and at the ready.

'Think we've found it, Putner.'

Putner stepped around and looked over the room; a chair, desk with a large radio set on it along with a note pad and metal ash tray, a cot bed in the corner. Putner moved past Snell and ran his hands over the radio like a hungry man stoking his lover's face. He flicked a few switches and checked the valves. He lifted the headphones and placed them over his ears. Silence. He tried another switch.

'You have experience with this type?'

'Not so different from the one we had back on the *Empire Carew*. Not working as it should.'

There was a candle in a holder on the desk and Putner lit it. Checking the drawers of the desk he located a small bag of tools. While Snell watched, Putner removed the cover from the radio set and began to check the innards of the machine. Snell looked back down the corridor wanting to be back and checking on the others.

'Go, sir,' said Putner without looking up. He took a hammer from the tool bag and laid it on the desk. 'I'll be fine – just send someone with food and cigarettes.'

Snell nodded.

'Good man. I'll send someone back to keep you company.'

Putner nodded absent-mindedly already absorbed in his work. Snell turned and headed back the way they had come. He stopped and looked back at the candle light flickering in the doorway and wondered if he was doing the right thing leaving one of his men alone. Nothing for it unless he wanted to wait here for Connelly or, worse, Busby to come and find them. Snell walked down the corridors and then down a ladder trying to remember the way that they had come from the mess.

* * *

The smell of frying fish reached Connelly's nose as they got closer to the mess.

'Jesus, that smells good.'

Busby grunted and they hurried on their way back. Footsteps on a ladder close by made them pull up. Connelly extended the blade on his clasp knife and the two sailors slipped quietly into the shadows at the edges of the corridor. They watched as Warner emerged from below decks, his bundle up on his shoulder like a seaman headed off for a long shore leave. Both men breathed a sigh of relief and stepped out of the shadows. Busby expected Warner to jump as they appeared but the man simply gave them both a cold, dead-eyed, look and nodded once before carrying on his way to the mess.

Connelly looked at Busby but the big sailor merely shrugged.

'Looks like he found a pair.'

'Maybe he had them all along.'

'Could just be.'

Back in the mess hall Earl Hamilton had got the stove going and was frying up the canned fish while he waited for the rice to cook, there were lanterns lit on the table, Collins lay on the furthest table with Amelia Starling sat close by him.

Warner dumped down his bundle. He tossed the cigarettes across to Lily, he retrieved one of the clay bottles and passed it to Busby before getting the whiskey out for himself.

'Any cups in this joint?'

Hamilton gestured with a wooden spatula to one of the bolted cupboards.

'Just tin cups, no fine crystal.'

'This isn't the kind of rot gut you need crystal for.'

Hamilton grinned.

'Mind pouring me a snifter?'

'Sure,' replied Warner.

Connelly studied the man; there was a tension in him that hadn't been there before, he moved with deliberate slowness, he stopped and turned feeling Connelly's eyes on him.

'You want a smoke, sailor?'

'Thanks.'

Connelly pushed a half-dozen of the Golden Bats into his pocket before placing one between his lips and lighting it.

'What happened to your shirt, Connie?' asked Lily.

Warner rounded on her.

'My name isn't fucking Connie – why don't you use my given name just one time, huh? Or is that too fucking difficult for you, you dumb fucking bitch?'

Lily's mouth formed an O in shock. Busby paused in his partaking of the sake.

'Watch your language when you speak to a lady.'

'Lady!' retorted Warner. 'I could tell you some things…'

Busby pushed the stopper back into the sake bottle and got to his feet, tattooed arms flexing.

'That so? Maybe I could tell you a thing or two as well, Mr Big-I-Am.'

Connelly watched Busby's stance shift ever so slightly and stepped between the men.

'Stressful time for us all here. You feel it? The strangeness? Let's all take a breath.'

'Oh, I'm breathing just fine, Mr Connelly.'

Connelly looked down and saw the cleaver that Warner held low.

'You don't want to do this. We all need to stick together. Three weeks in that boat didn't have us killing each other so let's not start now.'

Warner took a step forward and Busby did likewise. Everyone held their breath waiting for the next foot to fall. The sound of a hammer being cocked broke the silence. All eyes turned to Snell stood in the doorway.

'What is going on? Mr Busby, a step back, if you please, and Mr Warner please return that blade to the kitchen stock.'

Busby and Warner eyed each other but slowly obeyed Snell. Warner placed the cleaver on the table and then walked away towards where Collins sat, lighting a cigarette as he went. Busby looked at Connelly, shrugged, and then sat down and unstopped his bottle.

'What the hell is happening?' Snell asked Connelly.

'Nerves are frayed, sir.'

'Well, that's no need to be at each other's throats.'

Connelly smiled.

'It'll only get worse till we get picked up or make landfall. Just need to make sure we watch for it. There's something up with Warner, not sure what. Where's Putner?'

'We found the radio room but the set wasn't working. He stayed back to try and fix it while I checked on you – lucky I did.'

'Grub's up!' Hamilton banged his spatula against a tin plate. 'Come and get it while it's hot.'

They queued up quickly, plates in hand.

'Will someone take a plate to Putner when we're done eating?

'Not a problem,' replied Hamilton.

The food consisted of some of the canned fish fried with pickles and then mixed into the rice with generous portions of pepper and soy sauce. To the hungry company it was like mana from the gods and they ate like the starved people that they were, niceties and manners left far behind them – the Cafe du Paris could wait for another day.

* * *

The valves hummed, a needle flickered, and the radio set was lit up where it was meant to be. Putner put the headset over his ears, flicked a switch and was rewarded by the low hiss of white noise. He adjusted his dials and began to scan across the airwaves. Preferring to listen for surrounding traffic before he even thought about sending a message of his own.

He cruised along the dials stopping here and there when he thought that he heard something beneath the static. It was as though someone were trying to whisper to him when he had his head dunked in a tub full of water. More adjusting but still nothing he could make out. Punter leant back in his chair and took the headset off.

'Hey, Reg.'

Putner leapt up off his seat fumbling for the hammer on the desk. The heavy tool skipped away from Putner's fingers and fell onto the deck. Turning he saw Hamilton stood in the door holding a plate of food and two tin cups.

'Jesus, I could've brained you.'

'You'd need to pick up the hammer to do that,' Hamilton replied with a smile. 'Sit yourself down. I just brought you some food.'

'Food?'

Putner's eyes told Hamilton of the young man's hunger and he handed the plate across quickly. Putner sat down on the cot bed and Hamilton took the operator's chair.

'Brought us a couple of tots of whiskey too. Got some smokes as well.'

'Thanks,' replied Putner through a mouthful of fish and rice.

Hamilton chuckled and sat back letting Putner eat his fill before they talked. He looked the radio set over as he waited and wondered whether they could get any music through it – even Tokyo Rose on the Zero Hour would do, anything from the outside world. Just something to let him know that they weren't alone on an endless sea.

'I'll take that drink now – smoke as well if you don't mind?'

Hamilton smiled and passed Putner his tin cup. While the younger man took a hit, Hamilton lit two cigarettes and passed one across. Putner coughed from the whiskey and then took the proffered cigarette before taking a tote and coughing again.

'How's it going?'

'Well, the set's working.'

'But?'

'I'm not picking up much traffic. We need to decide if I send the distress signal or not.'

'Guess that'll be Mr Snell's call, not ours.'

Putner nodded and blew smoke into the air.

'What you going to do when we hit land?'

'A bath,' replied Putner, 'then send a dozen letters.'

'Who to?'

'My mother, my sisters, the company to make sure I get my leave and pay for time adrift!'

Hamilton smiled again.

'You?' asked Putner.

'A bar; hot music, rum, little band, some girls to talk to. Then food – let someone cook for me for a change. Maybe a walk on the beach and feel the sand between my toes. Finish it up with a sleep in a real bed; fresh sheets, soft mattress, and no one to wake me up – sleep till past noon.'

Putner extinguished his cigarette and took another hit from his cup.

'Well, I best get back to it.'

'You take the chair and I'll grab that cot while I finish my drink.'

They swapped places and Putner put the headset around his neck.

'Reckon I could come to that bar with you and get a beer?'

'Of course, man. We'll line the cold ones up.'

Putner smiled and went back to listening to the airwaves.

CHAPTER EIGHT

Lily watched Warner from across the room. The promoter and agent sat alone and smoked cigarette after cigarette while working his way through the bottle of cheap whiskey. She had been with Conrad Warner since the dark days of 1940 when it looked like Uncle Adolf was going to cross the channel and his legions would be goose stepping down Pall Mall. They had been through bad times as well as good and never once had he spoken to her in the way that he had earlier. Lily was still in shock from the venom of his words, so unlike the man she knew.

'Are you alright?'

Amelia Starling had come away from Collins and sat beside Lily. Lily looked at her and forced a smile.

'Not really. It's just all this I suppose.'

'He shouldn't have spoken to you like that.'

Lily took in a huge breath and blew it out.

'No, no he shouldn't have. We've chummed along for a few years now and I've never seen him like this.'

The two women looked across at where Conrad sat; yet another cigarette burning between his fingers, tin cup and whiskey bottle at his elbow.

'I suppose it hits us all in different ways,' proffered Amelia.

'Maybe. But I've been through some dark days with Connie and he's always been my rock.'

'Are you and he…'

Lily laughed, short and soft.

'No, but sometimes he talks like he'd want to but with Connie I'm never sure how much of it he puts on. I'll let him sleep it off and talk to him tomorrow.'

Snell had headed back to the radio room to speak with Putner and find out where Hamilton was. While Busby worked away at his bottle of sake, Connelly smoked and took out the book that he had stashed in his waistband. It was bound in cheap leather and looked like some kind of journal or day book. He wished that he could read the words within it. Connelly paused for a moment and then put down the book.

'Any of that sake left?'

Busby passed across the clay bottle and Connelly drained the last mouthful.

'Good book?'

'Might be but I can't read a bloody word of it.'

CHAPTER NINE

Every inch of your skin throbs, itches like the missing limb of an amputee. But with that comes an absence of pain. Sweet relief and you whisper your thanks for the cessation of the pain that has been your world for as long as you can remember. Was there anything before the pain? Out in the darkness something answers your words. The voices start as whispers and rise to a roar that hurts your ears. The voices press against your skull until they are within you – no longer speaking from out there but from in here, in your head. Are the voices yours or are you theirs? Who can tell but you begin to listen more closely now as they tell you what needs to be done. The mass of voices become one voice. His voice. And soon you are ready. Ready to slip out of your suit of skin and into another form.

* * *

Sleep had claimed Amelia. She lay face down on the mess table next to Lily. She wasn't sure what awoke her;

perhaps the roll of the ship, the crash of thunder outside, or some other unidentifiable thing that drags us back from the clutches of the sandman. But she sat up and rubbed her eyes, glad that her belly was still full and that she was out of the lifeboat. She looked around. Conrad Warner lay head down next to his empty whiskey bottle, Lily was leant in against Amelia's shoulder, Busby and Connelly had curled themselves up on the deck and were snoring loudly. She looked around to check on Collins with a feeling of guilt that she had slept while he had suffered.

He was gone. The mess table where he had lain was empty. The blankets they had covered him with lay on a heap on the floor beneath the table.

Amelia slid out of the bench seat and looked around the hall. He couldn't have got up – simply couldn't have. The man had been more than half dead. Where the hell is he? Thought Amelia. The mess hall was dark and silent, her rubber soled shoes made little noise, enough that it was drowned out by her heartbeat, as she crept around looking for a sign of what had happened to Collins.

* * *

'Do we send it?' asked Hamilton.

Snell stayed silent. This decision could save them or see them prisoners of the Japanese. He stared out of the port hole at the lashing rain. He turned and looked at Putner.

'You think anyone could find us in this storm?'

'Not likely, afterwards maybe, and I don't have our exact position – only the rough estimate that Connelly has given you.'

'Send it, you think?'

Putner shrugged.

'That's up to you, sir, but in this storm no one will be getting to us until it breaks.'

'Send it.'

Putner turned back and began to key in his Morse code signal.

…---…this is vessel Shinjuku Maru under British merchant navy control …---…assistance needed any other vessel please respond …---… this is vessel Shinjuku Maru under British merchant navy control …---…assistance needed any other vessel please respond …---…

'I'll keep sending and if anything comes back in I can vary it depending on who replies.'

'Can you tell a Jap from his code?'

'Maybe. There are ways to tell, ways they send messages and reply. I won't give out our position until I get something back.'

Snell nodded, happy that he had done all that he could. He took a cigarette from the stock on the table next to Putner and lit it up. The radio operator continued to tap-tap-tap away on his Morse key. Hamilton sat and watched the young officer wondering what was going on in his head.

'What next, sir?'

Snell turned and took a long drag on his smoke.

'Next? Next, we ride the storm out and hope an allied vessel picks up our signal. Until then we look after each other and keep together. I'm heading back over – are you coming or staying here?'

'Think I best come back with you and grab some shut eye before I get to thinking about cooking breakfast,' replied Hamilton.

Snell smiled.

'It's good to be able to eat again. How do you reckon to the supplies?'

'Reckon they've got more stashed but even with what we have I can stretch it for a week.'

'Good, good,' Snell extinguished his cigarette. 'Let's leave Putner to his work.'

Hamilton laid a hand on the radio operator's shoulder. Putner nodded without looking away from his dials, and Hamilton left with Snell.

* * *

Amelia gently laid a hand on Connelly's shoulder. He came awake in a second, clasp knife in his hand, blade extended with a simple movement of his thumb.

'Easy, Professor.'

'What is it?'

'Collins is gone.'

'Gone? How in the hell can he be gone?'

Amelia gave an exaggerated shrug.

'That's what I'd like to know – there is no way that he could be moving under his own steam. But he's gone, look,' she gestured at the empty table.

Looking up and down the mess hall, Connelly got himself up on his feet and tried to think.

'Maybe, he has managed to wander off – I've seen men do some strange things when they're hurting as bad as he must be.'

'No. There is not a chance that that man could have got up and walked away. This isn't adrenaline just after an accident. His body is ruined, destroyed. He hasn't been on his feet in close to three weeks. Not a bloody chance. We need to wake the others.'

Connelly saw the certainty on Amelia's face and he nodded.

'Well, however he has managed it we still need to find him.'

He kicked Busby in the foot and the big man sat up and stared murder for a moment.

'What?'

'Collins has vanished.'

'How the fuck has he managed that?'

'Not a clue but we need to find him.'

'Alright, let's get the rest of them up.'

With Conrad and Lily roused they set about deciding how best they should search for the missing Collins. Snell looked confused.

'How can he have gone anywhere?'

'I think we'll solve that when we find him, sir,' replied Connelly.

Hamilton rummaged in one of the cupboards and produced a pair of lanterns.

'Spotted these earlier, think they will help?'

'How many parties do we send out?' asked Snell.

Connelly thought for a moment.

'Just one. Everyone else stays here and keeps it secure. But what about Putner?'

'I could go and bring him back?' said Hamilton.

Connelly nodded.

'Alright, so if Mr Snell, me and Warner go out looking for Collins then Earl can go and get Putner and Busby you can keep Lily and Amelia company till we get back. Agreed?'

'I'd like to come with you, it could be Collins will need help if we find him,' said Amelia.

Snell nodded.

'I agree with Nurse Starling; she comes with us. Warner, you and Miss Cecil keep this room secure and Busby, I want you to go with Hamilton and collect Putner. I don't want anyone moving about alone. Then you return here. If we haven't found Collins in an hour we come back here and you three can go out on a different route.'

Snell looked around and let out a quiet sigh of relief when there was no disagreement. While Earl lit the lamps, Amelia checked the small medical kit. Busby scooped out a handful of the leftover food and ate the rice and fish out of his palm with the axe cocked back on his shoulder.

'How long till morning?' asked Lily.

Connelly threw a look out of a porthole but broiling cloud covered the sky.

'I'd reckon a good few hours yet.'

The ship shifted beneath them as it hit a heavy wave.

'Don't like being adrift like this,' said Busby, 'think I preferred it in the jolly boat.'

The others groaned at that.

'Best we get to it then,' said Snell, pistol in hand.

CHAPTER TEN

Beneath the hiss and crackle of the white noise, Putner was now convinced that he could hear voices, voices that chattered constantly. But still he struggled to make out individual words – was it in English? Who the hell would be transmitting like this? Without warning the radio waves went silent. Dead silent. Putner strained to hear amongst the nothing. Then he heard a voice; barely audible at first and then growing louder. His name whispered over and over again, first by one and then by a thousand voices speaking softly in unison.

'Reg. Reg. Reg. Reg. Reg…'

Putner tore the headset off and threw it at the cot bed. He stared at the castoff headphones but it was like after he had had an extremely long session on a set – it was as though he could still hear the voices chattering and bickering away in his ears; ghosts in the ears.

He stared at the radio set and lit a fresh smoke. He sat down on the cot bed. *Maybe I just need a bit of kip and then get back to it?* He smoked the cigarette down quickly and then stubbed it out before tucking the lumpy pillow behind him and leaning back on the cot.

* * *

'Where first?' asked Snell.

'The deck,' replied Connelly. 'Could be he wanted to feel the wind on his face one last time.'

Amelia took the lantern and Connelly took the lead. Keeping his pistol at the ready Snell brought up the rear.

Noise and lashing rain assailed them as soon as the bulk head door was open. The rain blew in on them in sheets that struck exposed flesh like bird shot. Connelly hugged the wall and Amelia got herself into his wake to shelter from the wind as best she could. Once he had the door shut Snell ducked low and followed, pausing only to push his pistol into his pocket where he hoped it would be safe from the elements. The filth on the deck had combined with the rain to make the surface as slippery and treacherous as walking across a greased pole at a fairground. They stepped gingerly but the deck shifted beneath them as the *Shinjiku Maru* rode the sea like a novice rodeo rider on the back of a bucking bronco. The waves were even darker than the sky and they hurled the powerless ship about with a furious anger, Neptune's wrath brought to bear.

'Up the ladder and we check the areas above,' Connelly shouted over the wind before turning and stepping onto the first rungs of the ladder that led up. He scrambled up, accustomed to the bad conditions; he had seen worse.

Amelia grabbed onto a rung and tried to grip the next with the hand that held the lantern. As she went to step onto the ladder the ship tilted suddenly and her weight was thrown back. The hand holding the lantern lost its grip and suddenly Amelia found herself gripping the ladder one handed – all her weight held by her hold on a wet rung. Connelly came back down at speed, seemingly as agile as a Barbary ape despite the slippery surfaces, and grabbed her wrist.

'I've got you. Give it a moment and the ship will right herself.'

The fear subsided in the young nurse and she was glad of the strong, vice-like, grip of Connelly around her wrist. The *Shinjuku Maru* suddenly righted and Connelly took the lantern from Amelia and they completed their ascent as Snell began his.

'Bloody bitch tried to throw me off!'

Connelly laughed. Amelia's cheeks were red and flushed.

'We'll have you talking like an old salt yet.'

She joined in with his laughter. A moment later Snell got up onto the deck.

'I can't believe that Collins could be out in this, not in his condition.'

'Agreed. Let's check these rooms anyway, never know what we might find.'

'Let's check the wheelhouse and then get out of this bloody weather. We can keep an eye open for other things while we search for Collins.'

They picked their steps carefully and made their way to the wheelhouse. Connelly stuck his head inside. Nothing looked to have moved since they had rifled through the room earlier. He turned to Snell and shook his head.

'He isn't in there. Let's check the other rooms up here.'

* * *

Back in the mess, silence reigned broken only occasionally by the crash of waves beyond the port holes. Lily sat and watched Conrad who sat with his head in his hands further down the mess table. She watched him but he did not once look up. He didn't even reach for a cigarette which was strange for him; as long as Lily had known him if he didn't have anything else to do with his hands then you could guarantee that he would busy them with lighting and smoking a cigarette.

'Penny for 'em?'

He remained with his face pressed into his palms.

'It can't be all that bad, we got out of that lifeboat, didn't we?'

Still no answer.

'Come on, Connie, I've never been one for letting a bloke give me the silent treatment and you've never been that type.'

His face turned out of his hands.

'What did I tell you about calling me that?'

'Now, don't start on that again – I've called you that since nineteen bloody forty!'

'What did I tell you? I didn't like it then and I sure don't like it any more now.'

'Maybe you should have said something back then then, *Connie*.'

Lily knew she was baiting him but anything was better than the cold silence that had reigned previously. He half came up from his sitting position and Lily followed suit her small hands clenching into fists.

'Don't even think about it. I've laid bigger men than you on their arses.'

Warner glared at her but didn't make a further move towards her.

'Oh, Lily. Lily, dear. If only you knew what there is in store for you,' his sad countenance split into an awful parody of a grin. 'The things they have been asking me to do to you... and me? Me, I've been sitting here telling them to shut up but you have to poke at me, don't you? Like a kid with a rotten tooth – you just can't help sticking your tongue in it.'

He reached for a cigarette then and Lily almost smiled.

'Who's telling you things? What the hell is happening to us?'

'Hell sounds about right, or maybe something much worse than that,' replied Warner as he shook his head as though trying to shake clear a fugue. 'God, I could do with another drink.'

He settled instead on getting up and taking a deep draught of water from the communal pot. While Warner's back was turned Lily picked up a short bladed knife that Hamilton had left on the worktop and slid it up her sleeve. She stubbed out her cigarette and continued to watch Warner.

* * *

Through dark corridors, Busby and Hamilton headed for the radio room. Hamilton threw a look back at Busby and was glad of the big man with him and the axe that he carried. Hell, he wouldn't want to run into Busby in a dark place and he knew the man.

'Alright?' Busby asked Hamilton and the cook nodded in response.

'Think I just got a touch of the heebie-jeebies.'

'Your lot get the shivers more than most. Ghoster'll do that to you.'

Hamilton ignored Busby's first comment and then replied.

'You been on one before?'

'Yes, over in your neck of the woods.'

'My neck of the woods?'

'Aye, in the Caribbean it was, Yank marines guarding the factories on account of the rebels and bandits. We were running bananas back to the states for United Fruit. A day out the Captain spotted a ship, drifting like. Me and three others got sent over for a gander. Took a jolly boat and rowed ourselves over. Strange feeling being on that ship adrift, everything left like the crew had just nipped off about other duties but they were nowhere to be found. I got the same feeling I'm getting here - got my hackles up.'

'Yeah, same here. Something real strange about this tub.'

'Hold up, is that the room?'

'Where the light's showing? Yeah, that's the radio room.'

'Alright, let's get Reg and head back.'

Hamilton pushed the door open. The room was in disarray; the chair overturned, blanket and sheet tossed from the cot, the radio smashed open and its innards spread across the desk.

'Busby…'

The big sailor had been waiting in the corridor but now he crowded into the radio room with Hamilton.

'What's happened here? Where's the lad?'

Busby looked around the room as though expecting to find an errant Japanese marine hiding in the confined space.

'This isn't good.'

'You can bloody say that again. Right. Back to the mess. We need to find the others and see if they've found anything, see if Reg has ended up back there.'

'Think there's someone else on board?'

Busby nodded.

'Starting to look that way isn't it. Reg wouldn't have been hard to take. Collins neither. Could be a couple of nips on here somewhere picking off the weak ones, like.' Busby suddenly banged his axe down on the table and Hamilton knew that he wouldn't want to be in the shoes of anyone that Busby found hiding on the ship.

CHAPTER ELEVEN

You cannot move. The ropes that bind you are expertly tied and every struggle simply tightens the intricate knots. You are but a hog, tied for slaughter. You are the last. None of your comrades could keep their heads. They have stripped you naked, bound you, and left you on the top deck. The breeze is warm but your lip quivers and your balls shrink back into you. He stands over you.

The priest in the conical hat leans down until his face is inches from your own. There is a scent to him; sickly and sweet like rotting apricots. He smiles and shows you his yellowed fangs. The priest points a finger at the sky and you follow his gesture. The sky above glows red and green behind the clouds. Behind one of the larger cloud banks you can see something, something huge – an eye here, a tentacle there, vast in both size and almost too vast for your mind to comprehend.

You look up at the priest and he points at himself.

'Kannushi! I am god master!'

He begins to laugh and draws a long knife from his robes. He reaches down for you and as the blade kisses your skin you wish you had died with your comrades.

* * *

'That door looks pretty solid,' commented Snell pointing out a door that lay ahead in the corridor that they were checking, 'could be something inside'

'You're right, let's check.'

Amelia was once again holding the lantern and was casting the light ahead of them. The glare of the lantern picked out something lying on the floor outside of the heavy door.

'What is that?' she asked.

'Looks like wet tissue paper,' replied Snell ducking to look further. 'Dear God!'

The young officer stood back up and took a step away from the object.

'What is it?' asked Connelly.

'I… That is, I think, that it's skin. Blood and skin.'

'Jesus,' Connelly took a closer look, 'wet too. So, it's fresh. Amelia?'

Ducking down on one knee, Amelia held the lantern close. She looked up at the two men and nodded.

'That's skin alright and I'd say it's human. The blood hasn't congealed at all. So, it is fresh…'

Snell brought up the Webley and pointed it at the door. Amelia scanned the corridor with the light of the lantern but not a thing stirred.

'Do the honours, Mr Connelly.'

Connelly got his clasp knife ready in his right hand and gripped the edge of the door with his left. The lock looked like it had been smashed off at some point. Connelly looked at Snell. The young officer tilted the cap back on his head and held his arm straight and steady.

'Now, if you please, Mr Connelly!'

Connelly threw open the door. Snell felt his heart hammer in his chest and then slow as the light from Amelia's lantern showed a small empty room. The walls were lined with wooden rifle racks, most of which appeared empty.

'It looks clear.'

Stepping around the door Connelly entered and looked at the rifle racks inside. It looked like some kind of ships armoury. There were still a few Arisaka Type 99 rifles left in the racks, they were the weapon that was employed by most of the Imperial Japanese forces. Connelly took one down from the rack and looked around for ammunition. He quickly located a crate filled with smaller boxes of 7.7mm bullets. There were other boxes next to the bullets but Connelly couldn't decipher the script on them. He flipped the cardboard lid of one and inspected the contents; beige waxy cylinders, about a foot in length and the width little more than that of a broom handle. Dynamite. Connelly turned away from the explosives and concentrated on the ammunition for the rifles that they had found. After stuffing a box under his shirt, Connelly loaded five rounds into the stripper clip and slotted it home. He worked the bolt to put a round into the chamber and then counted up the remaining rifles – there were five more. Connelly slung two over his back and Snell did the same. Amelia took the last rifle and likewise slung it over her back. They stuffed as many boxes of ammunition into their pockets as they could.

'Whose blood and skin was that?' asked Amelia, a shake in her voice.

'Collins?' ventured Snell.

'It really doesn't matter right now, does it? We have to get back to the others. See if they've seen anything when they got Putner. Strength in numbers and now we have these,' Connelly gestured at the rifles.

Snell nodded

'Agreed, let's go.'

Amelia sucked in a breath and nodded.

* * *

With the roll of the ship and the flash of lightning shadows leapt and elongated within the confined hallways of the Shinjuku Maru. The flickering light of the lantern merely adding to the effect. It looked as though sigils and signs had been smeared on the walls of the corridor with shit and blood. Hamilton stopped and squinted; ahead of them it looked like a figure moving across the head of the corridor, a silhouette back lit by the weak moonlight seeping in through the portholes.

'Busby…' he whispered.

Busby stopped and looked ahead. The shadow before them moved crab-like, scuttled as much as moved, hunched over and vanished across the junction.

'What the hell was that?'

'Who the hell, you mean. Gotta be whoever has been causing all this shit,' replied Busby and he dashed off ahead, axe held out before him. 'Show yourself, you bastard!' And with another roar he was off and following, moving in a fast loping gait.

'Busby, wait – shit.' Hamilton took another look at the graffiti scrawled on the walls. He looked back and Busby was gone around the corner. Hamilton took off after the big sailor.

* * *

Warner knelt in the corner of the mess, facing the bulkhead, rocking back and forth muttering to himself.

'No. No. No! I won't. I won't do it and you can't make me. No matter what. I. Will. Not. Do. That. Get out of my head! No. No,' he began to weep, softly at first and then louder. 'No, don't show me that. I can't do that. It, it's just too awful. Please. Please just be quiet. Let me think! Damn you, won't you just let me think.'

Lily had made sure that she stayed on the other side of the big table from Conrad. She looked over at him with every string of herself being tugged. She wanted to go and comfort him but she had seen the danger, the madness in his eyes. She prayed that the others would return soon.

Gradually Warner began to quiet. Lily smiled. Was he himself again? Had it passed? The weeping had stopped. She watched him from the corner of her eye. She watched as his shoulders relaxed and he gave them a flex. After a moment he rose to his feet, still facing the corner.

'Connie? Conrad? Are you alright?'

He turned and gave her a forced smile. He undid the cuffs on his shirt and rolled them up. After lighting a fresh cigarette he stood looking at her, the plastered-on grin still in place.

'What?' Lily asked.

'You know that I always loved you, don't you? Since that first time I saw you in The Royal Oak.'

Lily laughed.

'Don't be silly, you soppy sod, you just heard my voice and knew I could be your ticket to better things.'

The fake smile fell away and Warner's face took on a wan look.

'I wish I could've got up the guts to tell you, make you know. So much wasted time. I won't do it, Lily. I will not do it.'

'Do what, Connie?'

'What they want me to do.'

'What is it that they want you to do?'

Warner shrugged, extinguished his cigarette on the table and picked up a paring knife from the table. Lily stared at the blade. She had once had to cut a Maltese pimp across the face, after he had grabbed her up near Covent Garden, with a blade of a similar size. She straightened her arm and let her own knife drop into her hand from where she had hidden it in her sleeve. The handle felt angular and awkward in her grip. She looked at the knife in Warner's hand.

'What are you going to do with that, Connie?'

'I won't do it, Lily. I won't let them get you. Not through me.'

'Why don't you put that down.'

He offered out his arm to her and then slid the tip of the blade into his wrist with a gasp of pain. It was like nothing, just like a blade kissing the fat of a piece of pork right before you rub in the salt to make sure in crisps up right. He tightened his grip and then yanked the blade back towards himself lengthways down his arm and didn't stop until he reached his elbow. No smile now just a grimace. As his right arm blossomed crimson, Warner swapped the knife into his other hand.

'Connie! No, please!'

Lily scrambled across the table top. Warner shook his head and repeated the action on his left arm even as the colour began to leech out of him. Lily dropped the blade she was holding as she reached Warner. He sagged almost immediately.

'No, Connie, no. What have you done.'

She gripped the terrible tears in his arms in an attempt to hold the torn flesh together and blood ran between her fingers, wet and warm. So much blood. Warner slid towards the deck and Lily went with him. His white shirt was red now, Lily's hands too. His eyes flickered and his lips twisted into a familiar smile.

'Love you, my little cockney sparrow. Give me a kiss to remember you by?'

Lily leaned in and kissed him hard, tried to kiss the life back into lips that were already growing cold. Her tongue searched for his but Warner did not respond. She leant back and looked at his face; eyes closed, skin pale, but he looked more peaceful than Lily had seen him in the past few hours. The tears began to come hot and fast but Lily sniffed them back. She stood and looked down once at Warner's body in disbelief before stumbling away to find one of the remaining bottles of sake.

Benedict J. Jones

CHAPTER TWELVE

The corridors within the *Shinjuku Maru* proved to be like a maze and within half a minute of Busby taking off after the shade that they had seen, Earl Hamilton had lost him. Doors opened into cabins that opened into others. The corridors seemed strange, different from before. Hamilton stopped at a junction, four ways that Busby could have gone; straight on, right along another narrow corridor, down a ladder to the belly of the ship, or up another to the deck above.

'Shit,' muttered Hamilton as he stood and listened. The storm outside lashing the vessel made it hard to hear anything else.

In the end, he opted to head down the ladder. A quick check and then he would head back to find the others. Where the hell was Busby? Where was Putner? It was all going to hell and Hamilton didn't like it one bit. Below decks was even darker than above, there were no portholes here to provide natural light and the dingy glow of the lantern didn't seem like enough to hold the shadows back. Hamilton took another step and then a sound caught his ear. It sounded like a heavy footfall on the metal deck behind the closest bulkhead door. Hamilton paused, frozen to the spot, and listened for further sounds. None came and Hamilton gave a sigh of relief. Suddenly the pipes behind him began to clank rhythmically. Hamilton leapt against the bulkhead with his heart beating a swift tattoo. And then, despite the noise of the pipes, he could swear that he could hear voices on the other side of the door. Hamilton reached around and grasped the lever to open the door.

* * *

Lily bit back a sob and forced another bite of sake down. She fumbled on the table top and found a cigarette. Despite the shake in her hand she managed to get the smoke lit and took great long tugs on it.

'Why, Connie, why did you have to do that...'

She looked at her hands clutching the cigarette and the tin cup filled with Sake, stared at the drying blood that covered them. The tears threatened to come again but she would not allow herself. Instead she finished the smoke and threw back the last of the sake and felt it burn its way to her gut as she refilled her cup.

Behind her, Warner stirred.

* * *

Beyond the door, Hamilton realised he was in what had once been part of the hold, a large room that at some point had been used for refrigeration – to transport meat or fruit – but since then its usage must have changed. The room stank of piss, shit, stale sweat, and human fear. Hamilton gagged at the scent and covered his mouth with the hand that wasn't holding the lantern. From deep in the shadows of the chamber a laugh came. Hamilton turned towards the sound and, slipping his hand away from his mouth, he pulled the carving knife that he had tucked in his belt.

'Who's there?' he called, holding the lantern ahead of him.

Gradually a figure became visible; dark robes, large conical hat, hunched over and leaning on a long thin staff. The hat covered the figure's face.

'Who the hell are you?'

The figure looked up and Hamilton found himself staring into a pair of bloody, ruined, eye sockets. The orbs looked like they had been torn from out the sockets by talons or perhaps desperate, grasping fingernails. The rest of the face was pale and drawn, lined with age, and it ended in a slit of a mouth that split into a cruel grin. Hamilton felt the icy grip of terror close, like a hand, around his testicles.

'*Anata ga mietemasu*,' muttered the figure. *I can see you.*

Hamilton turned and headed back for the door at a stumbling run. As he got close to it, the door swung shut to reveal another figure who had been stood, hidden, behind it. The man was around the same height as Hamilton, he was naked and it looked like the skin had been peeled away from his body leaving him red and raw, dripping blood here and there. Hamilton stared closely at the flayed man and his ruined body and face, feeling the flare of recognition.

'Collins? Collins is that you?'

Collins opened his mouth to speak but he had no tongue anymore. Instead he opened his mouth wider than seemed possible and silently screamed at Earl Hamilton, the hacked stump of his tongue waggling, and then took a step towards him.

'Collins, you keep back you hear?' fear made Earl's voice crack.

Collins took another step and the man in the conical hat began to laugh again.

'I swear to God, Collins – you take one more step, man and I'll put this in you!'

Another step was taken and then another. Hamilton held up the lantern in a shaky hand to try and ward Collins off but the ruined man kept on coming.

'Don't make me, please don't make me – just step back.'

As Collins' foot hit the ground taking another step, Hamilton stepped forward and with a grunt pushed the carving knife in just below the ribs. It wasn't the first time that Hamilton had had to stab a man and he knew where to stick the blade so it didn't catch on the ribs. The carving knife slipped in easy, up to the hilt, ten inches of steel into the soft parts. Not a sign of it showed in Collins' face. He simply leaned to the side and then struck Hamilton across the cheek with a meaty backhand that sent the chef spinning away. The knife stayed stuck in Collins' side. Hamilton hit the deck hard and he could feel his cheek swelling up from the blow he had received. He turned and almost hurled the lantern but then fear of being caught in the dark with these two maniacs struck him. Instead he scrambled back and spidered across the floor looking for a weapon, looking for anything. Collins turned and with slow deliberate steps followed him. The priest continued to laugh.

Soon, Hamilton found himself backed into the corner with only his lantern. Collins continued to advance, taking his sweet time.

'BUSBY!' screamed Hamilton, 'BUSBY – help me!'

Realising help was unlikely, Hamilton struggled up after placing the lantern in the corner. Collins swung and Hamilton managed to block the blow with his left forearm, he snapped a jab back into the place where Collins' nose used to be. The punch had little effect and Hamilton followed it up by driving his knee into the knife handle jutting from Collins' side. The blade was driven deeper but no pain registered on the skinned man's torn features. Collins swung again and this one caught Hamilton in the jaw, smashing it with an audible crack and pushing bone through flesh. Hamilton dropped to his knees with his hands up to his face, pain blossoming. Collins stepped back and drove a punt into Hamilton's head that would have sent a rugby ball flying over the posts. The chef's head snapped back and bounced back against the steel bulkhead with a sickening crunch, muscles and ligaments twisted and tore in his neck. The lantern tipped and fell and the light was extinguished.

All that remained was the dark – and the priest's mocking laugh, as flesh slapped against flesh. It sounded like a beef carcass being hit by sledgehammers and Earl Hamilton was glad when sweet, sweet unconsciousness finally came.

* * *

As Lily lit another cigarette and tried to sort through the feelings that were raging within her, she failed to hear the first stumbling steps of Warner after he clambered to his feet. Warner's skin was as white as communion host, his shirt stained red, movements leaden, and his eyes as cold and dead as a corpse dragged from the river.

Just as Lily stubbed out her cigarette he reached for her. Something, some feeling, made her turn her head slightly and she saw the fist coming. Lily turned away enough that he only caught her a glancing blow across the back of the head. Ducking to the table she rolled clear and avoided the hammer blow that Warner slammed down with his fist.

'Connie?'

He stumbled towards her, movements as jerky as those of a marionette in the hands of a novice. She took a step back and stumbled, ending up sitting on the deck with Warner rapidly approaching.

'Connie, please – what are you doing?' she left unspoken, her wonder that he was even up and moving despite his pallor and the awful wounds in his arms.

As he closed on her, Lily waited until the final moment and then kicked out hard into the inside of Warner's left knee. Her heel connected solidly and his leg buckled. Scrambling beneath the table, Lily tried to crawl out to the other side but Warner grabbed her ankle and dragged her back. As soon as Lily's body became visible Warner drove a punch into her kidney, another dead centre on the bone of her spine, a hooking blow into her ribs that stole her wind, and another into the back of her head. Lily screamed. Warner tangled his fingers in her hair and turned her to face him.

'Connie, don't, please…'

She watched as he cocked his fist back and her hand leapt to the table, searching blindly. Lily had hoped to find a blade but instead her hand closed around the sake bottle. In the same moment that Warner drove his fist forward Lily smashed the bottle into the side of his head. Her blow had little effect and he followed through with his punch catching her, hard, above the right eye straight on the bone. Even as white stars danced before her eyes she could feel her eye swelling shut.

'Mnh, you bastard,' Lily's words were slurring now, 'my old nan hits harder than that. You fucking bastard. You're not Connie.'

The broken sake bottle was still in her hand and Lily drove the sharp shards of the clay bottle into Warner's eye – turning and twisting it once it tore flesh and the jelly of the eye into shreds. She felt a warm thick wetness ooze onto her hand. When Warner's grip on her hair still didn't release, Lily grabbed at his wrist, intending to drive her thumb nail into his wrist but instead it slipped inside his cold ruined flesh. Lily screamed again. Warner's fist pulled back and slammed a wicked hook into Lily's temple. She sagged, consciousness slipping but managed to return the punch with one straight into his face, breaking his nose. Another punch to the side of her head. Lily leaned forward and bit Warner in the chest. Bit hard until her teeth met. Nothing. He did not even flinch. *Jesus, what has he become*, she thought as she watched his fist cock back yet again. Darkness clouded the edges of her vision. *This one's the doozie*. But the blow did not connect. Lily struggled to focus but something was wrong. The fist wasn't there anymore. The thing that had been Warner turned and looked at the stump that his lower forearm had been turned into.

With a roar, Busby kicked Warner in the face and the force of the blow pushed him away from Lily, although his vice-like grip tore a chunk of her hair away as he was thrown back.

'You cunt,' Busby said as he raised his already bloodied axe, 'treat a fuckin' lady like that would you?'

Busby spat into Warner's face and planted another kick into his chin. He stepped back and set his legs. The axe dropped in a slow lazy arc and buried itself in the top of Warner's head. It was a murderous blow that shattered skull and hacked into brain but still Warner grabbed at Busby's wrist and dragged himself up. Busby reversed the axe and jammed the butt end into Warner's face hard but still he rose. The big sailor took a step back hardly able to believe that Warner was still coming.

Lily dragged herself up and grabbed a knife from the table. She turned and plunged the blade into Warner. He backhanded her across the face and she clattered to the deck. Busby pulled the axe back and readied himself. He held the axe two-handed near the end of the handle and stood like a lumberjack about to deal the final blow to some great redwood. He stared straight into Warner's eyes.

'Goodbye, *Connie*.'

The axe swung in an arc above Busby's head and then smashed through Warner's neck hacking into his spine and catching in the bone. With a grunt, Busby yanked it through. For a moment Warner stared at him with his cold dead eyes and then the final strands of skin and sinew gave, and his head bounced away beneath the mess table.

CHAPTER THIRTEEN

'Think we can make it back across the deck and down the ladder?' asked Snell.

Connelly stared out from their vantage point inside the doorway and took in the deep puddles, rain slicked surfaces, and the wind that was trying to shake loose even those objects that were tied down tight. He shook his head.

'Not something I'd want to chance especially loaded down as we are with these rifles.'

Amelia nodded.

'I don't fancy my chances, especially after last time. Shouldn't there be a ladder inside somewhere to take us down to the next deck?'

'Yes, sounds better than going out there.'

Connelly raised his rifle and Snell slammed shut the door. Amelia checked the action on her own rifle and followed. They moved by the meagre light thrown by the light of the lantern which Snell carried. The ship shifted beneath them as it rode a swell.

'It should be around here somewhere,' said Connelly as they made another turn. Suddenly he pulled up to a halt and his voice dropped to a whisper. 'Snell bring that lantern forward – I think there's someone down there.'

They were stood close to a ladder which led down, the ladder that they had been looking for. But in the inky, clinging, blackness of the corridor stood a shape. The light from the lantern reached the figure and revealed Putner stood against the wall. His hair was dishevelled, face pale, and posture hunched. But what drew their attention was his ears, or rather his lack of them. They were completely gone, dried blood giving him rusty sideburns and holes in the sides of his head where his ears had previously been.

'Reg? Reg, what the bloody hell has happened to you?'

The radio operator did not respond. Snell stepped forward pushing past Connelly.

'Putner – what's going on here? Where have you been and what the bloody heck has happened to you?'

Putner looked up as if it was only now that he had realised that they were there.

'They're coming,' he shouted rather than said it and Snell tried to hush him. 'They're coming!' Even louder.

And suddenly the corridor was filled with movement; the broken body of Hamilton stumbled into view, closely followed by the raw figure of Collins, and then others – bloated things, pale and damp, marked by scores of wounds, missing eyes, crabs clinging to their flesh in places. They looked like they belonged more to the sea than the earth which had borne them. There was something of the deep about them like catfish that Connelly had seen pulled up from the depths.

'Dear God, Jesus, Mary...' muttered Snell as he raised the Webley.

The things were moving slowly like they were unused to, and unsteady, being on the walk, as though their legs hadn't been used for some time.

'They're here!' shouted Putner and then he launched himself at Snell, snarling.

Snell turned and the Webley spat lead. The bullet tore a deep furrow along Putner's skull but he kept coming wrapping his hands around Snell's throat. Another shot rang out, Connelly throwing a round into the advancing throng to try and slow them. It seemed to have little effect.

'Help Snell,' he said to Amelia as he moved forward working the bolt on the rifle to chamber another round. The things before him were like creatures of folklore that had crawled forth from the pages of a book. Connelly aimed and shot one of the pale creatures through the head. The shot would've dropped a man but it barely slowed the creature, merely blowing a chunk of pale fresh from the skull. Connelly worked the bolt of the rifle.

The struggle between them had sent Snell and Putner to the deck. It was a desperate fight. Snell whipped the butt of the Webley across Putner's skull and the radio operator's hands squeezed, choking the air out of Snell, nails digging into the young officer's throat. The lantern rolled wildly. Amelia aimed her rifle at Putner's head but her finger froze. She could not do it, not to the young shy man that she had shared a lifeboat with for more than three weeks. She reversed the rifle and wielded it like a club. The steel butt plate connected solidly with Putner's skull knocking him sideways and giving Snell a moment's respite. That was all he needed – he tucked the Webley under Putner's chin and pulled the trigger splattering the ceiling with a spray of brain and skull.

Connelly aimed carefully and drilled a shot through one of the bloater's knees. Chambered another shot and swung up to aim at Hamilton.

'Earl – what's wrong with you? Help us man.'

The chef looked up, his skin looked like a crushed bag holding a pile of broken biscuits, with glassy blood shot eyes. Seeing no humanity in the look, Connelly fired. The bullet punched through Hamilton's shoulder but he and the rest of the horde continued. Connelly took a step back and then fired again taking little care with his aim.

'Back, we need to get back,' the fear was obvious in Connelly's voice. 'I can't stop them.'

'Out across the deck?' asked Amelia.

'We'll have to.'

Snell looked at the advancing figures.

'What are they?'

'I don't think we have time to ask them that now, sir.'

Snell raised the Webley and put a bullet through Collins. The man did not waver and simply continued to move forwards. They closed in like a wall of rotting flesh.

'My God.'

Connelly fired again, the bullet ricocheting from the bulkhead.

'Move!'

They moved back quickly. Snell had left the lantern where it lay and they moved through the darkness with only the portholes for illumination. Soon they were back at the door that led out to the deck. Connelly checked his rifle and then looked at the others.

'Snell, you're first. Get to the ladder and get down to secure the deck below. Amelia, once he goes down that ladder you count to thirty and then follow.'

'What will you be doing?' asked Amelia.

'Trying to buy us some time. Get down to the others and give them the rifles – looks like we have lost Putner and Hamilton, Collins too. But that should still leave six of us unless anything else has happened.'

Snell simply nodded, his mind reeling from what they had just encountered. Connelly unslung the other rifle from his back and made sure that both were fully loaded. The sound of shuffling steps along the corridor told him that it wouldn't be long.

* * *

Busby and Lily sat on one of the benches in the mess, Warner's decapitated corpse lying close by. The bloodied axe lay on the bench at Busby's side. They smoked in silence until Busby spoke.

'I've seen some strange things over the years. Seen lights in the sky in the far north, seen lizards as big as dragons, knew a man once who swore he had heard a mermaid sing near the Falklands. And once, I saw a voodoo procession near Port au Prince and the people moved like he did just then, like they had lost something that made them like the rest of us. Hightailed it out of there that time. Scared the shit out of me.'

'I've never seen anything like that. Never,' replied Lily. 'Connie was dead. I know he was dead – he opened up his wrists in front of me. He was dead - no two ways about it, but he got up. He was dead and he got up.'

Busby shook his head.

'It's this ship. Something's wrong with her. Felt wrong from the off. I don't know where she has been, or why, but I know it's wrong. I can feel it and if it wasn't for the storm I'd want to get back in that jolly boat and cast off, take our chances.'

'But in the storm?'

'I doubt we would last ten minutes in that little tub out in this. Wouldn't do it unless there isn't any other choice.'

'So we wait for the others – and then?'

Busby shrugged. Sounds reached their ears.

'Is that thunder?' asked Lily, and Busby grinned.

'Not like any thunder I've ever heard. Sounds like gun fire to me.'

'Snell?'

'Could be but that was a lot of shots and it sounded more like rifles to me. It's stopped now.'

Busby's fingers stroked the haft of the axe on the bench next to him and its solidness comforted him.

* * *

'Now!' shouted Connelly and Snell moved off through the door and onto the storm lashed deck.

Connelly stayed low and moved out around the corner. They were still coming, moving slowly but still quick enough that they would be on them within a minute or so. Putner was back up, shattered head hanging to one side. *Time to slow them down a bit more*, thought Connelly. Each of the Arisaka Type 99 rifles held five rounds. Connelly picked up the first rifle and he aimed low. He fired off all five rounds in quick succession at knee height. He dropped the empty rifle and picked up the second repeating the action until it too was empty. Bullets into the creatures might not have had any real effect but knees and shins that caught rounds still caused the bloating creatures to stumble and fall gaining them time as they were forced to right themselves. Connelly pulled himself back around the corner and began to reload stripper clips into the rifles.

'He made the ladder yet?'

'Just getting there,' replied Amelia.

'As soon as he goes down you start moving across the deck. Don't bother counting.'

She stared at Connelly and nodded.

'Just make sure you're three steps behind me, sailor.'

* * *

The deck beneath his feet was even more treacherous than Snell could have imagined; at a village fete he had once run across a greased pole above a pit of muddy water – this was worse. The rifles slung across his back seemed to tug him to one side while the wind pushed his legs to the other, threatening to hurl him to the deck. Lightning flashed and the rain blew in in sheets. Snell risked a glance backwards and saw Amelia's face in the doorway. He looked up and saw a man stood high up on the top deck. The lightning flashed again and the priest stared down at Snell. The young officer fumbled for his pocket and his revolver. Thunder rolled directly above the ship and beneath the sound Snell heard another - a loud twang. The sound was odd and out of place. He didn't see the cable coming, sprung free and twisting in the air like a terrible metal serpent. The line struck Snell just above the left elbow and smashed through flesh and bone. Snell screamed and barely heard it as the thunder rolled again. His arm clutching the lantern hit the deck. Snell made a grab for it but the ship pitched and his severed limb was cast away across the deck. He stumbled forward and his momentum carried him towards the ladder leading down. Grabbing at the rail to slow himself, Snell felt the butt of his pistol clash against the metal and his fingers slip Suddenly his feet were over nothing and with another cry, he dropped down the ladder, fast, to the steel deck below.

Amelia was up and moving. She ran across the deck feeling the rubber soles of her tennis shoes sliding. She watched as the cable lashed out again. Throwing herself to the deck, she slid on her stomach and the cable snapped above where her body had been a mere second before. She continued to slide until she managed to get a hand around a rail. With grunts of effort, Amelia dragged herself towards the ladder still lying on her belly with the rainwater soaking from the deck and through her uniform, which damply hugged her. When she reached the ladder, she looked down and saw Snell in a crumpled heap at the bottom.

'Damn,' she adjusted her grip and then grabbed onto the ladder and swung herself onto it, determined the ship would not throw her no matter how much it shifted and bucked.

* * *

They were so close now that Connelly could smell them; rotten fish, decayed flesh, and the wet smell of the sea on a warm night. He scuttled back to the door and watched Amelia crawling back towards the ladder. The first creature turned the corner. It was a fat slug of a thing, hugely bloated in the gut, ragged remnants of white shorts clung to its legs, and the green of sea weed showed tangled amongst its wet hair. Connelly snap fired and the shot missed its mark. He shouldered the rifle and fired the next four shots in a tight pattern into the creature's face. Stepping forward, he used the butt of the rifle to push it back into its company. Hands grabbed for him and Connelly leapt back. Time to go. He slung both rifles and ran for the door and was out into the storm. The rain stung his face and the winds plucked at his clothes. He slowed his pace and picked his way gingerly across the deck towards the ladder.

CHAPTER FOURTEEN

Two clanging knocks sounded on the outer door of the mess. Busby turned, hand closing around the handle of his axe and he got up. Lily reached a hand out and laid her fingers upon his arm.

'It could be the others,' said Lily.

'Could be,' replied Busby, 'but then it could be someone else instead, couldn't it?'

Lily picked up a knife and they headed to the door together.

'On three,' said Busby and Lily nodded. 'One. Two. Three.'

He threw the door open and raised his axe one handed. He looked down and saw Amelia down on the deck with Snell. Busby took in the missing arm, makeshift tourniquet, and the pale face of the young cadet officer. Busby dropped his axe and scooped Snell up from the deck in his big arms.

'Where's the professor?'

'Behind me.'

'Was that rifle fire earlier?'

'Yes, they attacked us.'

'They?' asked Lily.

'Hamilton, Putner, Collins, and… and other things.'

As Busby lay Snell down on the table and Amelia stripped the two rifles from off her back Connelly reached the door. He stepped in and dragged the door shut before locking it.

'Busby, get that other door locked.'

The big sailor nodded and moved off to lock the room down. Amelia stole a glance at the doors. She wondered if they would hold out the dreadful creatures they had seen above and even if they did how would they escape from this floating prison. Once Busby had the other door secured he turned to Connelly.

'So, what's this all about, professor?'

Connelly shook his head but then looked up and spoke.

'It's the ship, it has to be. It's madness. I don't know where this ship has come from, nor where it has been, or what port it calls home but there's something wrong with it. Plain and simple it's a hell ship, cursed.'

'I pretty much said the same thing without getting attacked by anything,' replied Busby.

'Something that makes dead men stand up?' asked Lily pointing to Warner's corpse.

'I don't know. I'm not sure I believe my own eyes after what came at as just now. Dead men and then some.'

Snell moaned in pain and Amelia went to check on him.

'What did you tie the tourniquet with?' asked Connelly.

Amelia looked up and gave a grim smile.

'My brassiere, it was all I had to hand.'

'So what now?' asked Busby as he picked up one of the Arisakas and loaded it. He passed the rifle to Lily and then loaded another for himself 'I'll run through the basics with you in a minute.'

Connelly was surprised at how soft Busby's voice was when he spoke to Lily.

'Now, I think we have to get off this bloody hell ship as soon as we can.'

'You think *they* will let us? asked Amelia nodding her head upwards.

Busby collected up his axe.

'Miss Starling, I couldn't give a flying fuck what those bastards want, pardon my French.'

Snell coughed and pushed himself up on his remaining elbow.

'Language, Mr Busby, there are ladies present.'

Busby laughed.

'How are you feeling, sir?'

Jesus, thought Snell, *it must be bad he called me sir and sounded like he meant it.*

'We can't leave this tub afloat. What if another boat stumbles across it? Or worse, what if someone tries to take it into port? No. We need to send the *Shinjuku Maru* down into the deep. Scuttle it.'

The pipes around the room began to clank and clang. Snell looked at them.

'Sounds like she doesn't want us to do that.'

'There're explosives back in the armoury. There were other boxes, I took a quick glance in. Dynamite, I reckon. Busby, would you have any idea where we should put charges to scuttle a ship?'

The big sailor smiled.

'Oh, I reckon I can manage that.'

'So it's settled?' asked Snell. 'We scuttle the ship and take to the boat?'

Nods all round.

'Rather take my chances back in the lifeboat.'

'And send those things down with her,' threw in Amelia.

'Send her down and let the waters wash the evil away,' said Connelly finally.

* * *

Once Snell's arm was tightly bandaged Amelia fashioned a sling for him from a slashed-up blanket. Busby put a full load into the Webley and put the pistol into Snell's right hand.

'There you go, sir.'

Snell nodded and the rest of the company took in how pale he was. The young man's eyes opened.

'Put my cap on for me won't you, Busby?'

Busby picked up the cap and put it on Snell's head at a jaunty angle.

'Think you're just taking the piss now, sir,' Busby said in a voice low enough that only the two of them could hear.

'Maybe, I am - just a little…' he closed his eyes and took a deep breath. 'Have I done alright, Busby?'

'More than alright, sir. We've made a proper officer out of you, we have. The captain would be proud, your father too. I'd be proud to serve on any ship with you as master.'

'And I'd be honoured to have you with me, Mr Busby.'

Snell smiled and the others gathered up their rifles. Connelly loaded up the two spares and passed one to Busby while slinging one across his own back.

'We might be glad of the extra shots.'

'Aye,' replied Busby likewise putting one of the rifles on his back. 'Professor, you know the way back to this armoury so you lead and we'll follow. The ladies will stay with Mr Snell and I'll make sure no one comes at us from behind. No lights, we don't want them to see us coming.'

'No lights,' echoed the others.

Connelly grabbed the handle on the door and the others brought up their guns. A clunk of the lock and the door swung open showing the dark corridor beyond. Nothing stirred. Connelly led the way moving in a half crouch with his rifle tight into his shoulder and levelled at the darkness. Snell kept his pistol pointed at the deck and followed slowly. Lily and Amelia held their unfamiliar rifles pointed down and Busby brought up the rear with his axe in his right hand and rifle in his left.

The pipes that lined the corridors clunked and throbbed as they moved through the shadows and murk. Connelly threw a glance at them and then went back to watching ahead of him – with every step he expected to see pale flesh emerge from one of the doors that lined the corridor but there was nothing. He put one foot in front of the other and the rest of the group followed tightly in his wake.

At the turn in the corridor that led to the armoury Connelly raised a hand to halt the others and risked a quick look around the corner. Everything was quiet apart from the roar of the storm outside. Connelly turned and Busby crept up close.

'How do you want to do this?'

'In and out. What we are looking forward is in a pile of boxes behind the ammo.'

'You got any experience using explosives?'

'A little – not much, you?'

'Thought you Irish lads knew all about bombs…' Busby smirked and Connelly ignored him.

'I shipped with a fella who had been down Mexico way after the last war helping some revolutionaries or some such. Had a long trip with him and he tried to show me a couple of things. We'll wing it somehow. Tell the others to wait here while we get the boxes.'

'Alright, professor.'

Once the message had been passed the two sailors crept around the corner and headed for the armoury.

'Too quiet,' whispered Busby and Connelly silently nodded back.

Connelly got to his feet at the door while Busby remained low. As Connelly's hand closed around the handle the electric lights along the corridor began to flicker on.

'What the hell?' Busby stood and the lights went on full no longer flickering 'How has the ship got her power back? She was dead in the water.'

But before they had time to discuss the matter further, the other doors along the corridor swung open. Pale shapes piled out of the doorways, more than a dozen of them. They were moving faster than they had been previously, climbing over each other as they attempted to get to Busby and Connelly. Busby fired off the five shots in his rifle and then hurled it at them before readying his axe. Connelly got the door open before turning and shooting one of the creatures in the face. He turned and looked back towards where the others were with thoughts of getting them all safe behind the heavy door. More of the pale shuffling man-things had cut off their retreat and amongst them Connelly saw his former shipmates; Collins, Putner, and Hamilton.

'Busby!'

The big man turned and saw what was happening. He shoved Connelly roughly into the armoury.

'Get in there! Do what needs to be done, sailor.'

He pushed the door shut and spun the lock before turning to where the others were.

'Collins! You still owe me money you rat bastard!'

Lily aimed her rifle and put a shot into the gut of the closest bloater. The bullet pierced the flesh releasing the scent of saltwater and death. The rifle kicked back hard into her shoulder and she struggled to work the unfamiliar mechanism of the bolt. Amelia fired at the monstrously misshapen head and swiftly chambered another round, the rifle not being too unlike the one that she used back home on the farm.

'Bullets slide off them like butter from corn.'

Snell fired the Webley.

'We need to get back.'

'But the others?' shouted Lily.

'Bloody hell,' Snell shoved his pistol into the face of the oncoming creature and pulled the trigger taking off half its face. From out of the mob a hand grabbed

Snell's wrist and yanked him forward. It was Putner. He raised a hand and slammed his fist down into Snell's face. Snell raised his non-existent left hand to try and ward off the attack. The flayed Collins leapt in and his teeth bit down on the bandages covering Snell's stump. Snell screamed and triggered the Webley into the seething mass of stinking flesh that was enveloping him. Collins bit down harder and came back up with a mouthful of blood. Punches struck Snell about the face and he struggled to get the Webley up again.

Amelia and Lily fired in unison and then took a step back. Snell had vanished amongst the oncoming mass. They looked desperately for him but all that remained was his cap lying on the floor.

'Back,' muttered Lily. 'We have to get back.'

She fired again and took two steps back. Amelia looked again for Snell but then did likewise. The mass came on and they took another step back. The wall of rotting flesh swelled towards them and they turned and moved back fast the way that they had come.

Busby threw an arm around the neck of one of the bulbous walking corpses and yanked back hard enough to break the neck of a normal man. But the dead thing was no normal man and as his spinal column snapped his sea-sodden head tore free from the mooring of his neck. Busby cast it aside and swung his axe hacking a pathway for himself. He grunted as the heavy blade smashed through limbs and hacked into flesh. Busby looked up and watched as Snell went down under the weight of his attackers.

'No,' he said simply.

He saw Putner crouched down, raining blows into Snell's head and Collins crouched with blood around his mouth grabbing at the stump. Busby threw up an animal cry like some primal berserker and shouldered his way through the other grabbing things with elbows and axe swinging.

'Collins!'

The flayed creature looked up from gnawing at Snell's wounded arm, some recognition dawning though the fugue in what remained of his mind. He looked up blankly at Busby in the second before the head of the axe smashed into his face. Busby gave the handle a yank but it was stuck fast in Collin's skull. He let go and kicked the flayed man away. He turned to Putner and smiled, hand edging up his back.

'Here, hold this for me, Reg...'

Busby pressed the button on his stiletto and the blade jumped into place. He stabbed the blade in low catching Putner in the groin and then pulled his arm up with all the force that he had. The stiletto opened Putner up from groin to rib cage before the blade caught in bone. Busby followed it up with a haymaker of a left that knocked the radio operator off his feet. One of the washed-up dead grabbed Busby about the waist and slammed him into the wall of the corridor. Busby tossed the stiletto into his left, raised his right arm, and stabbed back into the creature's face peppering it with wounds. A normal man would have had to release but the creature simply squeezed the bear hug tighter. Busby snarled and continued to stab out.

On the floor beneath them, Snell looked up and saw the struggle. He spat blood and raised the Webley tucking it in behind the knee of the shambling corpse. He pulled the trigger and the big .455 bullet severed the monster's leg dropping him, and Busby, to the deck.

Busby got himself turned around and smashed his fists into the water bloated face until the head came apart beneath him. Another hand grabbed at him but he swayed away and pulled Snell up.

'Time to go, sir.'

CHAPTER FIFTEEN

Inside the armoury, Connelly locked the door. He heard the hands beating on the other side of it but knew that it was strong enough to hold. The electric light blazed away through the bulb in the ceiling and Connelly was glad that he didn't have to spark a match in the presence of explosives. Looking around the room it was easy enough to locate the boxes that he had disregarded earlier. He opened the first and stared inside. It was packed with beige sticks that Connelly had recognised earlier as dynamite. He searched through the boxes and found a variety of fuses and timers. These went into one of his trouser pockets and he stuffed four sticks into the other. Another half-dozen went down the front of his shirt. Not enough. *Unless I touch it off here*, he thought, *need a way out first and to warn the others if they're still alive.* Connelly looked around the room and his eyes lighted on the ventilation grill in the far corner of the room the boxes beneath forming an easy staircase. Connelly weighed a box of the dynamite in his arms – *not too bad.*

He checked that the box would fit and then removed the grill. Once it was down he checked that there was enough squeeze space to jam himself into the duct behind the box. There was. He turned and went back to the other boxes checking the fuses as he went and trying to remember all that he had been told on a long hot voyage.

* * *

Lily pulled up against the wall of the corridor and looked back. No one was following - yet. Amelia was already pushing off ahead further into the darkness.

'Come on!'

'Where are we going?'

'The boat, we make for the boat and if any of them got through that they will meet us there.'

'Shit,' Lily pushed off the wall and stumbled on, 'you think they did?'

'I don't know. I hope they all got clear, but...'

Lily didn't reply. She knew exactly what Amelia meant. They had seen Snell go down and there had not seemed any hope for him, likewise Busby and Connelly cut off by the crowd of bodies. Lily took a deep breath and followed with her hands tight around her rifle.

* * *

The wind and rain hadn't dropped down at all. Busby pushed himself in against the wall and carried Snell along the slippery deck.

'We'll be alright, sir. We'll get to the boat. No need to worry now. Be back in Ceylon in a few days. I'll get you back, sir.'

Snell was silent, semi-conscious, his body battered and stump bleeding. Busby carried him as one might carry a new born, he took careful steps and picked his way along the deck, light of foot for a big man. The lightning flashed further out at sea and the thunder rolled above them. Busby looked out at the dark waves and longed to be on them instead of on the cursed ship on which he stood. The rifle across his shoulders felt heavy. A door opened ahead of him. He turned and another opened behind. Figures filled the night. Busby laid Snell down on the wet deck.

'You stay there, rest easy, sir, I'll be back in a bit.'

In the lightning flashes he saw Hamilton ahead of him with three or four of the bloaters behind him. He turned and looked back – Collins stood, axe still in his face, with Putner next to him. Putner's intestines hung out of him like a nest of snakes.

'Right you bastards – who's first?'

The roar of the sea was the only reply. Busby slipped the rifle off his back and knowing the bullets were next to useless against the fiends, he wielded it by the barrel like a cudgel. Busby ran down towards Hamilton. He swung the rifle with enough force that as it connected the stock splintered and shattered into matchwood. Hamilton's head hung broken and Busby swung the rifle back catching him again and knocking him sideways. He reversed the remnants of the rifle and stabbed it into the gut of the first bloater. A clammy fist slammed into his nose and Busby felt it break. It wasn't the first time that had happened and he shrugged it off with a sniff before twisting the broken weapon in the creature's guts. He let go and pulled his already extended switchblade from the back of his waistband. Two slashes across the face opened up the already stretched flesh. Nails clawed their way downs his face and blood blossomed. Busby pushed against them trying to force them into the rail and over the side. A huge left hand knocked him back and they came on.

'Shit,' Busby turned and ran back towards Snell, stumbling on the deck.

Collins reached down and Putner tried to reach around him to get at Snell. Snell's eyes opened and his right hand shot up to grab the axe buried in Collins' face. He yanked it clear and with a twirl hacked down to take off the front of Collin's foot. Reversing the axe, he pushed the heavy head into Collins and moved him back.

A second later and Busby got back to them. He dropped the knife and grabbed Collins between the legs with his right hand, left gripping his shoulder. He lifted the skinned man bodily and cast him over the rail. Putner came up from the deck.

'You next, Reg.'

Putner looked at Busby and then stabbed out with the stiletto that he had collected from the deck. The blade bit deep and Busby roared. He grabbed Putner's wrist and smashed a massive right hook into him that knocked his head sideways. Slipping Putner's head beneath his left arm in a headlock Busby grabbed at his belt and once he had a grip he tossed him over the side.

Busby looked down and saw the blood leaking out of him.

'Ah, shit…'

'Busby?'

'Sir?'

'Get clear, I'm done. Leave me and save yourself.'

'Respectfully, shut the fuck up – sir.'

Busby pulled the knife out of his gut. The blood was black in the moonlight. Busby laughed to himself and then turned to face the remaining attackers.

* * *

The boat was as they had left it. Busby's knots had kept it lashed tight to the posts. Lily looked around and while Amelia kept watch she began to hack through the knots with the knife that she had kept from the kitchen. The knots were sodden with rainwater and they proved hard to cut through and so she moved on to simply cutting the lines themselves which wasn't much easier. Amelia stood guard while Lily worked, the rifle held across the crook of her arm.

'We can't go yet, Lily.'

'Why?'

'I can't go, not if they might still be alive. We'd be leaving them here with those things.'

Lily worked the blade of her knife through another knot and knew that Amelia was right. But still she continued to work, she spoke as she cut.

'And how will we know? We can't go back in there after them. How long do we wait?'

'We wait, I don't know how long – as long as we can I suppose.'

Amelia looked back at the door into the ship.

'Come on, professor, come on,' she whispered.

* * *

Connelly wormed his way through the air vents. They were just too narrow for him to move comfortably. Instead he pushed the box onwards and then wiggled his shoulders to move forwards. It was slow going but he pushed on. Once he reached another of the ventilation grills he paused and stared through into the darkness below. Something pale moved at the edge of his vision and he held his breath for a moment until the shade passed before he pushed and wriggled, pushed and wriggled, and made his way forward.

Eventually he reached another grill through which he saw nothing. He pushed the box further on and worked his way past the grill before slamming his heel into it and knocking it out of place. He pulled the box back towards him and then dropped down bringing it with him. Where were the others? Would they have headed for the boat? No time for any more chances not if the fuses back in the armoury worked like Connelly hoped they would. A movement at the edge of Connelly's vision caused him to hurl himself to the side. The priest's staff missed him by inches. Connelly pulled his clasp knife and thumbed the bade out. The priest watched him with blind eyes from the shadows cast by his conical hat.

'Last dance,' said Connelly. 'Time running down — tick-tock, tick-tock, tick-tock.'

The priest jabbed out with his staff and Connelly swayed back. He kicked out with his foot and the hunch-backed priest leapt away with a speed that belied the look of him. Connelly reversed the knife so that it pointed downwards from his fist.

'Come on, you little shit.'

A grin in response and the staff lanced out, it caught Connelly in the shoulder and knocked him off balance the priest spun it back and cracked the wood across Connelly's face. He stumbled and the priest closed in. Connelly tried to shake the pain of his cheek from his head. He let the priest close in and then reached out. He grabbed a fistful of robes and pulled the priest onto the blade. It cut deep straight into his chest where his bastard heart should've been. Connelly pulled back his head and butted the priest in the eye. The blade came out and then slipped in again through the priest's neck; Connelly gave it a twist. The priest began to laugh and Connelly shoved him away. He reached into the box and pulled out a stick of dynamite that he had already fed with a fuse. The priest reversed his staff and ran at Connelly. In the moment before the staff stabbed into him, Connelly saw that the end was sharpened like a primitive spear. Impaled upon the staff, Connelly screamed as it punched through him. The priest ran him across the room and with every step the makeshift lance pushed further through the sailor. He grabbed for the priest's head, knocking off the conical hat and got the bald nut-like head in his grasp. With a scream that was half agony and half battle cry he bounced the priest's head off the wall and then threw him back. Waves of pain like nothing he had felt before hit Connelly, combining with the alien feeling of having something through his body that didn't belong there.

Connelly turned and pressed the butt end of the staff against the wall. He pushed himself against it and forced his way down the length. He could feel the rough wood inside him and every inch was agony.

He looked over and saw the priest climbing back to his feet. Connelly dragged his body to the end of the staff. He heard the suck and squelch of blood and torn flesh as he dragged himself along it and he could feel the splinters of wood dragging at his insides. He pulled on, and then reaching around his back, he managed to wiggle the shaft loose from him. The priest was up now. With a scream Connelly hurled the staff away and fumbled the matches from his pocket. The first match snapped but the second sparked and Connelly touched it to the fuse of the dynamite stick.

'Here, have this.'

Connelly leapt forward and shoved the lit stick down the front of the priest's robes. He grabbed a hold and swung the smaller man until he had some momentum and then let go casting him down a stairwell. He left the box of dynamite where it lay and stumbled away as he counted off the seconds in his head. Every second he counted seemed to coincide with the drip-drip of blood falling from him.

CHAPTER SIXTEEN

Busby felt the ship shift beneath him. But this was no roll of the sea, it felt like the wheel had been turned and the ship cast in another direction. Looking out over the rail Busby could see that the sky looked different where they were headed – even through the rain he could see the torn space they were headed for. The light itself seemed different there as though the fabric of their world had been ripped open and another made visible.

On the deck, Snell sat with his pistol in his hand. The creatures had them penned in now. Snell fired his last shot through a pale head and then Busby leapt forward slashing and cutting through flesh. Fists hammered into the big sailor, body and head, as he cut at them. Busby threw a vicious left in response and hands grabbed at him. He could feel the strength beginning to fall away from him.

'Shit,' he cut at the hands that held him but the grip was tight.

Snell broke open the revolver and placed it between his legs as he emptied the shells out and then reached for the fresh ones in his jacket pocket. Not many left now. Snapping the Webley shut, Snell raised the pistol and fired shot after shot in the beasts that were trying to drag Busby down. A low thump sounded somewhere on the ship. Busby smiled and then felt the bones in his arm give under the pressure of the hands, like chalk beneath a boot heel. He screamed and sliced at them with the knife but there were too many now and more hands grabbed at his knife. A fist slammed into his face like a brick and Busby felt his front teeth go, another caught him across the jaw and he heard the snap. Snell fumbled with the pistol and loaded his last two bullets in. Teeth bit down tearing the flesh in Busby's neck. The big man screamed again and tried to get one of his arms free but it was no use they had him tight. He felt teeth snap through his ham string but couldn't even lift his leg to stamp down.

'Mr Busby!'

Busby felt more teeth biting into his flesh, fingers tearing soft parts away, but he managed to turn. Snell aimed straight at Busby's head. The big sailor closed his eyes and Snell pulled the trigger. Busby sagged amongst the horde and Snell turned the gun back on himself. He put the barrel in his mouth and squeezed the trigger again.

* * *

Connelly slipped and fell to the deck. He saw the puddle beneath him cloud red as his life leaked out into it.

'Ah, shit.'

He forced himself up and looked around to re-orientate himself. *Close now, the boat can't be far.* With a deep groan, he pushed on with stumbling steps. *How long has it been? How long left on those fuses?* He slid rather than climbed down the ladder and his knees hit with a violent jolt. He saw Lily and Amelia and stumbled towards them.

'Professor!'

Amelia caught his arm.

'There isn't time. Get the boat into the water. Get yourselves in.'

'But you're hurt…'

'No time. I've set the dynamite. Not sure how long we have left. Get the boat out into the water.'

The two women manhandled the boat over the side and slid it into the crashing waves. Lily jumped down but Amelia turned back to Connelly.

'Get in the fucking boat, Nurse Starling.'

She wiped back a tear and leapt down. With effort Connelly stood. He risked a look back and saw them, the bloated dead thing, coming along the upper deck. He turned and flopped down into the boat. He struck his leg on a bench but barely felt the pain.

'Push off with the hooks. Get us clear.'

Lily strained against the hook to push off but the waves quickly grabbed the little boat and cast it out to sea, away from the *Shinjuku Maru*. Waves slammed against the little boat and water sprayed over the trio huddled together.

Connelly coughed and blood stained his chin.

'Sit me up.'

They got him up and sitting, and he watched the ship as they moved further and further away. When it came, it was nothing like you would expect. It was audible rather than optical; there was a loud thump that could be heard even over the noise of the storm. The *Shinjuku Maru* shifted and leaned to one side as it raced for the tear in the horizon.

'Go down you bitch,' muttered Lily.

The ship listed heavily to one side and then turned so far towards them that the funnels faced out at the retreating lifeboat. And then it was gone.

'We did it, professor! We beat it – we won.'

Amelia turned, smiling, and saw that Connelly's eyes were closed.

EPILOGUE

The Catalina seaplane flew another circle and then came in slow and easy to land on the calm blue ocean. The sky was a deep azure. It took the crew some minutes to prepare a dinghy and send it out to investigate the lifeboat that they had spotted from above.

Two crewman paddled the dinghy over while others watched the sky and sea and manned the Vickers K machine guns that bristled from the big seaplane.

'Reckon we'll find anyone this time?'

The other crewman shrugged.

'As long as it isn't another body job.'

They pulled alongside. Inside the lifeboat a shelter had been rigged using the sail and formed a tent around the rudder.

'Ahoy, the boat,' called the first crewman while the other withdrew a Webley revolver from his holster, 'anyone alive in there?'

The sail shifted and moved and then opened. A head stared out at them, an unruly mass of sun bleached blonde hair atop it.

'Took your bloody time didn't you?' asked Lily.

Another head appeared and Amelia looked out at them.

'Just you two?'

They looked at each and nodded. The crewman tied up alongside and got them into the dinghy before rowing back for the Catalina. The plane was locked down and the dinghy stowed away. Lily and Amelia were given mugs of hot sweet tea and put into seats like passengers with somewhere to be. The Catalina began its run and got into the air like a fat duck.

Beneath them the calm sea bubbled here and there. A water-logged corpse popped to the surface. Then another. Another. And another. They sprouted like mushrooms in the dark places. The sky began to darken and lightning flared in the distance.

'Something up with the radio, Captain – hearing some right strange things…'

HELL SHIP

AUTHOR'S NOTE

While the events depicted in Hell Ship are completely fictional they were inspired by the massacres of the crew and passengers of the ships The Behar and Tjisalak by the Imperial Japanese Navy during the Second World War.

This story was, in some way, my way of trying to make sense of such acts. May we never forget the inhumanity that man has inflicted on his fellow man, in the hope that such things never happen again.

ABOUT THE AUTHOR

Benedict J. Jones is a writer of crime, horror, and
westerns from south-east London.

He is probably best known for the Charlie Bars series of
neo-noir novels and for the splatter punk novella
Slaughter Beach.

The Sinister Horror Company is an independent UK publisher of genre fiction founded by Daniel Marc Chant and J R Park. Their mission a simple one – to write, publish and launch innovative and exciting genre fiction by themselves and others.

For further information on the Sinister Horror Company visit:

SinisterHorrorCompany.com
Facebook.com/sinisterhorrorcompany
Twitter @SinisterHC

SINISTERHORRORCOMPANY.COM